Scorched Earth

Glenn Haybittle

CHEYNE
WALK

"Music was my refuge. I could crawl into the space between the notes and curl my back to loneliness."

— Maya Angelou

"The first peace, which is the most important, is that which comes within the souls of people when they realize their relationship, their oneness with the universe and all its powers, and when they realize at the center of the universe dwells the Great Spirit, and that its center is really everywhere, it is within each of us."

— Black Elk

Sam

1

He stares at himself in the mirror and says his name aloud. "Sam Pearson." He feels his face and the contents of his mind don't quite relate to each other, as if each speaks a language unknown to the other. Sometimes he thinks there is nothing more guaranteed to alienate you from yourself than pronouncing your name aloud while looking at your face in a mirror. It can be like summoning forth the full frightening magnitude of the unsolvable strangeness of life.

"Sam Pearson," he says to the glass. Now his voice, like his face, seems to belong to a stranger. A blank-faced perplexed stranger awaiting the next moment of his life, doubtful it will ever arrive. He can pull up no defining radiance of personality onto his features, into his voice. How far down into himself does he have to go before he understands who he is? He makes some grotesque faces. His face in the glass, he realises, is leading him now. He feels like his face is following the cues of his reflection, mimicking its prompts. The thought begins to frighten him. As if madness is at hand, never very far from the surface.

To inhabit his body and face with more surety he thinks of things he knows about himself. His favourite food: crisps and chips. His favourite TV show: *Star Trek*. His favourite occupation: playing his bass guitar. But soon he finds himself thinking about things he doesn't like about himself. The constant sensation he has in public that everyone is looking critically at him which makes him as self-consciously awkward as a novice on skis. He doesn't like that. And he doesn't like how much thought he can't help giving to potential mishaps whenever he is tasked with performing an errand. He pictures calamities and his imagination brings them to the brink of fruition. He doesn't like how, whenever a teacher singles him out in class, his blood catches fire and he has to dig his nails into his palms to stay in his body, to stop the alarming sensation of floating up towards the ceiling like a fugitive hot air balloon. He often sits with both his legs and feet crossed, his arms folded, making of his body a roughshod double spiral. It's a way of making himself feel more compact, like a parcel ready for mailing. Because he doesn't feel compact at all. He feels all his component parts haven't been competently welded together. As if any jolt in the road will loosen all the hinges and joints. As if any jolt in the road will unravel him.

Sam is thirteen. His mother named him after a film star, but she is now at a loss to remember who that film star might be. No one at school calls him Sam. At school he is often known as Straws because of his thin legs and arms. Jones, Dixon and Warlow call him Samantha. Because they think he's more like a girl than a boy. Or else they call him Muppet. And now Jones, very pleased with himself, has started calling him Aids. Sam had to google Aids because he didn't understand the hidden code of the insult Jones was directing at him. Even after googling it he can't say he understands what Jones means. Not that it matters what words Jones uses to insult him. The expression on his face is eloquent of his opinion of Sam. It's one of the few moments in his life when Jones achieves eloquence. He is good at contempt. Much better than he is at English, History or Science. And Dixon and Warlow imitate everything Jones does. Often they try to outdo him, as if Jones is a sexy girl they are showing off for. Recently their persecution of him has precipitated because Sam made overtures to befriend Jamal, the very shy Syrian refugee boy who has joined their class. Manifestations of vulnerability, loneliness, always summon in Sam a protective instinct. Jamal's loneliness was so apparent he felt compelled to reach out and offer some kindness. Jones, Dixon and Warlow call Jamil "the terrorist". But they don't physically hurt Jamil. Instead they have begun physically hurting Sam. They are testing how far they can go, what degree of violence they can get away with. Every day it gets a little worse. Even when Sam is not at school they are like three sleek shadowed sharks circling in the waters of his mind. Sometimes he fantasises that he is granted super powers. Then he vanquishes all three of them in a dazzling feat of ingenuity in the school playground and everyone stares at him with startled admiration.

Sam lives in fear and dread of each new school day. He lies awake in bed at night willing the hours to pass more slowly. It frightens him sometimes to think about time and how we can never escape the tight clasp of its companionship. To give himself courage he watches YouTube videos of the 1980s band Orfée. He feels protected for as long as every song lasts. Both taken out of himself and taken more deeply into himself where fear can't reach him. It's the bass player Nick Swallow who reinforces his desire to go on living. Something about his appearance, the way he projects himself out into the world, thrills Sam. Nick Swallow provides him with a blueprint of how he might become more harmonised inside his body one day. Sam has been playing bass guitar for two years. His bass guitar is his best friend, his only friend. It feels like he is fulfilling a need of his nature when he is playing his guitar, as he imagines a bee must feel when settling itself between the yielding petals of a pollen-heavy flower. He is learning all of Nick Swallow's bass lines, one by one. He has mastered all the bass lines on *Fingerprints*, Orfée's first album. Nick Swallow's technical ability improves impressively on the second album, *Climbing Trees*, and provides challenges which Sam relishes. But he can't go on studying Nick Swallow videos all night. He knows you mustn't wear out the things that bring you comfort. And then the shrivelling dread of spending another day at school returns. Sometimes he worries he might end up imitating his father. Once, when he was no longer able to hold back the tears in front of his mother, his stepfather stepped in and chided him. "If you don't man up you'll end up like your father." His mother gave his stepfather a look of reproach. His father has been edited out of every narrative in the new family home. His stepfather broke a rule by mentioning him. His stepfather is an actor. Sam has seen the film in which his stepfather plays the hapless drunken victim of a werewolf. He only had one line. Sam felt a guilty rush of support for the werewolf when it eyed his stepfather and bared its sharp teeth. Now, his stepfather is very proud of his new acting role as a violent husband in a primetime soap opera. Sam always shuffles off to his bedroom when it's on television. Jones, Dixon and Warlow deploy his stepfather and his bad acting as another taunt.

Sam's real father jumped in front of a train when Sam was five. He has never been able to learn from his mother why he did this. He imagines his father must have been deeply unhappy. He fears he might have been weak. His father's surname was Wyatt. Sometimes in the mirror he calls himself Sam Wyatt. Sometimes at night he thinks he detects the presence of the shadow of his father in his bedroom.

Sam made the mistake of telling a girl at school what happened to his father. Natasha, an overweight girl with mottled skin and crooked teeth. He didn't believe she was capable of treachery because barely anyone ever speaks to her. A week later, Jones had the information. It's now another of the taunts he directs at Sam. One time he and Warlow enacted the moment of his father's death. Warlow jumped down from a desk, arms flailing, and Jones played the part of the train, thumping into Warlow and knocking him to the ground. There's nothing more dangerous, more frightening and more likely to escalate into the spread of violence than cruelty. Sam knows this. Once cruelty is aroused in one person it begins to infect others. It's why he values kindness above all other qualities. It's why acts of kindness can bring him close to tears. Cruelty is the comprehensive absence of kindness. Cruelty is what he understands as the devil. And kindness is what he understands as God.

Recently Sam has discovered he has a second self. This second self is a shade wiser than Sam and sometimes answers his questions.

"Do you think we ought to steal some money from mum's purse?"

"Why not? How else are we going to feed the fox?"

His second self though has no answer to Jones, Dixon and Warlow.

Sam has considered various options for evading school. He has imagined hiding out all day in the local cemetery. Or better still, spending all day with his grandmother who has dementia. His family say the person she once was has vanished. They are all unsettled that she no longer recognises them, as if their vanity is offended. It doesn't bother Sam that she doesn't know his name. He has trouble himself answering to his name. He goes to see her every day after school so that his grandfather can go out for a walk and do some shopping. He enjoys the atmosphere she creates around herself. He finds she allows him to be himself, without inhibitions. He feels a kind of solidarity with her. She too has been forced into exile from a truer life. Sometimes she turns away from him and begins to talk to someone only she can see. She talks to people no one else can see most of the day, every day. Just like he talks to Nick Swallow and his second self who no one else can see.

His grandmother was once a ballerina. Whenever he goes to see her the first thing he does is to fit one of the buds of his headphones into her ear and then perform some improvised madcap dance moves for her which she almost always copies. Music always lifts her spirits. She wears a wide smile when they dance together. Usually she copies all his movements, but now and again she performs a few movements he recognises as belonging to classical ballet, mostly gestures with her arms and hands. When she does this, she possesses more poise and grace than anyone he knows.

Sam has two ambitions. One is to learn to play the bass as well as Nick Swallow. The other is to do a project about his grandmother's career as a ballerina.

2

"Yeah, you should be loving someone. Oh, oh. Loving someone."
Sam sings this at the top of his voice to his grandmother and
points at her. It seems to please her. She is quick at taking pleasure in things. So he sings it again.

"Over and over," says his grandmother. It's become her
mantra. She says *over and over* whenever her eyes lose the light
that make them her eyes.

"Who's that?" says Sam, pointing to a black and white photo,
fingerprinted and curled and yellowed at the edges, of five young
people locking arms on a railway station. He has foraged this and
other old photographs from a cardboard box of memorabilia.
It is packed with old photos, newspaper articles, programmes,
train tickets, letters and even a pair of pink ballet shoes.

"I don't know. I lose sight of the lights."

"That's you. When you were seventeen."

"I don't think so." She looks pained for a moment, as if someone is twisting her wrist.

"You need to believe what I say to you. I don't tell you lies.
Well, sometimes I do. I told you yesterday that Leonardo da
Vinci was flying over from Italy to have dinner with you. But
that made you happy, didn't it? You said what a nice man he
sounded even if you didn't know who he was. This photo was
taken during the war. In 1940. You were part of a dance company and you're about to go to Holland. Your mother had to
chaperone you because you were so young. Your dad wouldn't
allow you to go but he was away in the RAF and your mum

disobeyed his orders. And when you were in The Hague, Hitler attacked Holland. You stood on the roof of your hotel and watched German soldiers falling down from the sky. You had to escape Holland in a boat. And the queen was in another boat not far behind." Sam knows all this because his grandfather has told him. "That was incredibly brave of you. Going through all that when you were so young. I wish I was that brave."

"Have you seen my friend? She didn't come yesterday, but I think she's coming today. She always wears a silver dress. Sometimes she brings me flowers."

"Do you mean her?" he says, pointing to a girl in the photo.

His grandmother twists a silver ring with a green stone round and round her finger. It's like she is trying to summon a magic power from it. Then she looks up and over at the window. "Look at all the people in that tree. What are they doing?"

"They must be fairies. I think they're waiting for you to dance. They've heard what a brilliant dancer you were."

"There was a man in my room today with a twisted face and he kept hissing at me. I don't want to see him again."

"Oh him. I've sent him away. I packed him off in a taxi. I gave him a one-way ticket to Australia."

"Did you really? Thank you. He was frightening me. I like it when people are kind. I like your face. You've got a kind face. I like people's faces when you can see kindness in them. Some people's faces have no kindness in them. I don't like those kind of faces."

"There are three boys in my class like that. They don't know how to be kind. Or they think being kind is the same thing as being cissy. They make my life hell."

She is the only person he's able to confide in. She, like he feels himself to be, is an outcast of society. With his mother he feels constrained to downplay all his troubles. Because she makes him feel she already has a weighty burden to carry.

"Over and over and over." She spider-crawls both her hands over the table in a straight line and counts to ten until her arms are fully extended. Her expression at times resembles that of someone who has recently traipsed across a war-torn border on foot, but he is often conscious of how beautiful his grandmother's hands are, how much vitality they still convey.

"Look at this photo. That's you with Margot Fontaine. Were you good friends?"

"Margot? Is Margot here?"

"Do you remember her?"

He fancies he can almost see how slowly, how arduously her brain works.

"Is my father still upstairs?"

"No, he left the world a long time ago."

"They will be sorry they missed me. They don't really understand what happened. I reached up as high as I could."

"I know you did."

"Is that what she said? I couldn't understand her."

"Let's dance again."

She stares at him as if he is something just pulled out from a magician's sleeve. The thought makes him feel guilty, but the madder his grandmother becomes the more he likes her. The more space she grants him to find and be himself. Of all his family she is the only one in whose achievements he takes pride. As if she might be a beacon for his own aspirations. Before she "lost her marbles" as his stepfather puts it, she was an admirable rather than a lovable woman. She stood aloof. Her diction was precise, her words eloquent, but she withheld feeling from everything she said and touched. His own mother always gives her a low rating as a mother. "About two out of ten. There was barely a single maternal instinct to be found in her. She never allowed me to see the grain under the paint. I can't remember her hugging me once in her entire life." To Sam, whose mother's hugs always seem more duty-bound than heartfelt and make him squirm with discomfort, this doesn't seem such a bad thing. And whatever his mother thinks, he knows his grandmother still wants love and feels love like anyone else.

"Shall I read you tonight's pudding menu?" He picks up an electricity bill from the counter and performs his best impersonation of a diligent waiter. "Okay, tonight you can have boiled and deep fried and marinated hippopotamus earlobes or else you can have chocolate pudding with custard."

She laughs. "Chocolate pudding and custard," she says.

3

Confrontation number one: Fifty more yards until he reaches the school gates. He is dragging his feet. A knotted pain in the pit of his stomach. Blood throbbing in his wrists. The inside of his head like a Mediterranean hotel room –every noise too loud, every noise loaded with jarring echoes.

They seem to take form out of his fraught imagination. As if his fear has bodied them forth. Warlow with his spotty sepulchral face and darting snake eyes and scrawny overcharged body. Dixon with his grazed hands, his boxer shuffle and dismal smell of gravy. Jones with his comedian's eyebrows, his cruel mouth and strutting imperious show of masculinity. It's eloquent of how unhappy Sam is that they are the most pulse-quickening presences in his life. More so than Nick Swallow. More so than his grandmother. Warlow snatches his bag, rips out a page of his geography homework, screws it up in a ball and forces it into Sam's mouth. Jones looks on approvingly. Then they saunter off laughing. The attacks never last long. They are careful to leave few clues at the crime scene.

Confrontation number two: He is sitting next to Jamil in the canteen. Jamil is still polite, still struggling with his English, but never now initiates any contact with Sam. As if he's realised Sam is at the bottom of the food chain and any alliance with him puts him at more risk to every lurking predator. "The terrorist and his lover boy," says Jones as he walks past. He cuffs Sam's head. Sam sees two of the girls on the other side of the table find this amusing. It's always demoralising to discover girls too can be cruel. All the girls at the table have refused his Facebook friend request. It never occurred to him in his initial surge of enthusiasm for gathering friends that people he knows and sees every day would snub his invitation. It was how he discovered the extent to which he is a laughing stock at school. He has five Facebook friends, three of whom are complete strangers. The only time anyone posts anything on his profile page it is to mock him. He has come to detest Facebook. It has brought more hate into his life.

Warlow now picks up his plastic plate of pasta and pushes it into Sam's face. "Whoops. Sorry," he says. "I slipped." The girls laugh again. Sam acts as though nothing out of the ordinary has taken place. He fights down the urge to cry. His second self tells him to be brave. He discreetly cleans his face with a napkin. And feels Jamil edge further away from him.

Confrontation number three: They are waiting for him outside the school gate. Warlow trips him up from behind. Sam falls to the pavement. A bus rumbles past. He catches the eye of a woman with tightly-pressed thin lips looking at him through the greasy window. Her face offers no moral support. While he is sprawled out on the ground, Jones yanks off one of his shoes and walks away with it. Sam gets to his feet. The feeling that everyone is looking at him more acute than ever. A voice calls out to him from behind. It's a Muslim boy called Waseem from the year above.

"Yeah, what's up little man. Why you let them step on your toes like that, man? They be owning you. Listen, a blud got to be fighting his own fights, innit. But I seen you be welcoming to our Syrian brother and I be respecting that. So I be giving you some intel. You got to be taking out the weakest link. It be bait, man. You got to brain the scrawny chief. You feeling me?"

Even in his agitated humiliated state it strikes Sam with how much rhythm Waseem scans his sentences. He finds himself imagining a bass line he might deploy to accompany Waseem's words.

"What does brain mean?" he asks.

"Slap him, brud. Single him the fuck out and hit him with your best shot. I be waiting and watching."

"Thanks," says Sam. He doesn't know how to reciprocate the elaborate dance of hands he has seen Waseem exchange with his friends so when Waseem offers his hand Sam can come up with nothing more affectionate or thankful than an old-fashioned handshake.

4

Sam sits in his bedroom with his bass plugged into his 30-watt Marshall amp. He is watching a YouTube video of Orfée performing 'The Frozen Time' live at the Hammersmith Odeon. Trying to copy every note Nick Swallow plays. He still can't master the thrilling bass lines in the song. But he's getting there. And, as always, Nick Swallow gives him courage. Sometimes he wishes he could let Nick Swallow know how much courage he gives him. But to imagine any kind of communication with Nick Swallow is to own the full magnitude of his insignificance in the world.

He is in trouble with his mum for returning home wearing only one shoe. She repeatedly shook her head in wearied disbelief while rebuking him. He had to tell her more lies. He is too ashamed of his weakness, too reluctant to add to the burden his mother makes him feel she carries to admit he is being bullied. Jones, Warlow and Dixon, he realises, force him to live in a house of deceit. The deceit, like a rampant virulent weed, is beginning to overrun everything within him that is true. At dinner she tells his stepfather the story of the missing shoe.

"You're turning into a bit of a lost cause, aren't you, son?"

At ten o'clock Sam creeps downstairs in his socks. His mother and stepfather are watching television. The volume is loud because his stepfather is hard of hearing, even though he refuses to ever admit this, refuses to acknowledge any signal of vulnerability. There is a surge of dramatic music as he walks past the closed living room door. Sam enters the kitchen. It still smells of the earlier microwaved dinner, except the aroma has grown still more sickly and stale. He opens the back door. The patio security light clicks on. The fox, as always, is sitting six feet away, staring intently at him. She looks so gentle. Even trusting. And yet Sam knows she is capable of savagery. He wonders if there is something he might learn from her. He would like to be as skilled as her at hiding from the world. He is flattered that she leaves her hiding place to seek him out every night. He knows it is the food she wants, but, even so, he feels he has earned her trust to some degree. Every week he spends some of his pocket money on food for the fox. Tonight he has nothing of his own to give her. So he steals two of his stepfather's sausage rolls from the fridge. His stepfather has forbidden him to feed the fox. He says foxes carry disease. One night he caught Sam in the act of feeding the fox and chased it off with an ostentatious show of bravado. He suspects his stepfather enjoys doing things that make him dislike him. Just as Sam enjoys infringing on his stepfather's laws.

He crouches down in the doorway and holds out his offering to the fox. The fox locks eyes with him. It's the look in her eyes that makes him feel sure she is a female. He wonders if all species of females have a different look in their eyes to males, like they have different genitals. Something he's never thought of or observed before. There's a moment of heightened communion. The fox makes him a larger mystery to himself. Makes of the moment something clean and radiant and far-reaching. Behind her the form of a tree, welling out of shadow, raked by silvery particles of light, is a bewitching breathing presence under the stars, a lighted canopy of stillness. He can feel the pulse of both the fox and the tree dwelling in him too. As if an intimate connection has been established. He feels privileged to be sharing this moment together. He doesn't want the spell to end. But he hears a movement in the house and quickly tosses the two sausage rolls onto the patio and closes the door.

Back in his bedroom he recalls Waseem's kindness. He

doesn't think he has it in him to hit anyone. But he doesn't want to let Waseem down. It's an important part of who he is to repay kindness. He realises it's Warlow he hates the most of his three persecutors. Now and again he glimpses something in Jones which makes him think they could be friends if Jones dropped his guard, took off his hard-man pantomime mask. He knows Jones' father is in prison. He knows Jones' father is a loud-mouthed thug. A man whose self-esteem resides almost entirely in his ability to physically intimidate other men. He knows Jones looks up to his father. And he knows Jones would be a better person if he didn't look up to his father. Sometimes he thinks Jones hates him because Jones can read his mind and secretly knows he is right. Sometimes he thinks Jones hates him because he sees something of himself in Sam which he can't allow himself to admit if he wants to go on receiving the approval of his father. Sam has no desire to ever be Warlow's friend. Warlow, he suspects, would be capable of leading women and children to a gas chamber if he believed it would make him feel more important to himself.

He props a pillow on top of his bookcase and, half-heartedly, he pretends it's Warlow's face and practices throwing a punch at it. The first punch he has ever thrown in his life. He wants to admit defeat, but his second self tells him to try again. He listens to Nick Swallow's bass playing on Orfée songs on his headphones while delivering a series of slack indecisive blows to the pillow. "Picture Warlow in a Nazi uniform," says his second self. Sam obeys and sees Warlow's hateful sneering face with greater clarity. There is an increase of vigour, of willed malice in his punches now. Heat rises from his torso. He hears Warlow's sharp whiny voice in his head. It's good to make fun of the way our enemies talk. It makes us feel a little taller, a little broader across the chest.

The muscles in his thin arm ache and the joints in his shoulders throb when he gets into bed. But under his duvet, the light of a streetlamp falling close to his face, he is once again convinced he won't be able to go through with the challenge Waseem has set him and there's nothing his second self can say to make him change his mind. He begins to will on an illness. He relishes illness. Spending all day alone in bed. The respite it provides from making decisions, from taking responsibility for his life.

5

The disembodying sensation that everyone is looking at him is still more pronounced at school the next day. The secret he carries in his mind makes him feel he is conspicuously aglow. Only he knows what might happen to Warlow today and it's true what they say that knowledge is power. But it's a power he struggles to own or make use of, like a foreign language no one else speaks. Every time he catches Warlow's eye, there is fear in Sam, but there is also a feeling that he has acquired an advantage which reduces Warlow to his rightful size. Ignorance, Sam understands now, shrinks people. Ignorance makes people make more noise to appear bigger. Like his stepfather. But most of the noise his stepfather makes is just bluster. If the fox bared her teeth and began chasing him, Sam is almost certain his stepfather would run away. Today he has to be the fox and hope Warlow runs away when he bares his teeth.

In history class, while they are learning more about Hitler, Himmler and the Holocaust, Warlow flicks an elastic band at him. It stings his cheek. Without meaning to, Sam makes a tight fist of his hand. He enjoys the sensation of the warm rush of blood in his arm. But not the panicked thump of his heart afterwards.

At lunchtime Warlow throws something at him. It hits him on the mouth, a slimy wet thing, and lands next to his yoghurt on the table.

"Warlow has just had a wank in the toilet," Jones tells the girls.

It's a used condom. Its utterly incongruous presence electrifies the entire table. The girls all stare at the thing aghast. Sam has only ever seen a condom once before. In a park. A dead and sordid thing. And yet to his thirteen-year-old mind the whole force and mystery of life seemed to stream through it. Nothing he's seen since has been so eloquent of the thrilling and terrifying mysteries of life.

He realises he could probably get Warlow expelled for what he has just done. There were lots of witnesses. And the evidence sits leaking creamy sauce before him on the table. It would be a way out of standing up for himself, of asserting his rebellion, of excavating within himself the audacity to throw a punch at Warlow. For a moment he considers walking over to one of the teachers. But he knows how much everyone hates a snitch. Knows, as a snitch, he would be singled out for still more mockery, torment and violence.

All afternoon he notices Warlow never strays more than three feet away from Jones and Dixon. It's the first clear sign of weakness he has detected in Warlow. But every time he imagines marching over to Warlow his heart threatens to explode in his chest.

Out in the corridor, between the final two classes, shoes squeak on the tiles and voices are raised in the momentary release from enforced constraint. Sam is resigned to admitting yet another defeat when Waseem appears. He winks at Sam, then throws an arm around Jones and another around Dixon. He escorts them away. Warlow tries to follow, but Waseem wags a finger at him. Everything Waseem does seems a flowing part of a single unifying choreography, like how Sam imagines his grandmother when she danced. Warlow is now standing alone. He looks peeved, suddenly unsure of himself. For courage, Sam summons up an image of Nick Swallow in his mind, his slightly sinister android smirk. And he visualises the act of punching Warlow. His second self tells him he can do this. His second self urges him into action. Sam imagines his father must have visualised the act of throwing himself in front of the train before he did it. He knows his father must have put himself in a trance before jumping. With his head full of these thoughts and under the influence of his second self, he strides over to Warlow and hits him in the face. He performs the act in a dream-state. As if it is still something he is imagining. It isn't a good punch, doesn't make any kind of meaty connection. There is no crunch of bone or cartilage, but the blow stuns Warlow. Sam hits him again. There's more of the dislike he feels for Warlow in this punch. Warlow now fights back. Sam discovers how much emotion explodes inside you when you're hit in the face. A crowd gathers around them. They are grappling on the floor when a teacher arrives to break up the fight. As he's marched off with Warlow, Sam sees Jones. Jones has a smirk on his face, but a smirk with new meaning. It almost resembles Nick Swallow's onstage smirk.

Nick

1

Half an hour ago she had been a he. Her new body caused her no more distress than her old one had. It had already solicited propositions from a succession of gloating, foul-mouthed, barrel-chested males. If she was surprised by the persistent attention she attracted she hid it well.

The night sky to which she paid no attention contained some unblinking galactic debris, but there was no turbulence in the atmosphere to make the stars wink. She arrived at the entrance of a shopping mall, a formal composition of sharp edges, rinsed acrylic colours and thin vinyl outlines. Figures were hovering in groups of two and three – shining-faced, conscience-clean youngsters with a jittery quality about them as if they were all waiting for an authority figure to arrive. All the girls flaunted an identical look, as if there were only one mutually agreed upon way for a female to be beautiful - tanned adolescent skin, wide highly-sexed mouths, bee-stung lips, high chiselled cheek bones, a mane of black or blonde hair in post-coital disarray. They all wore high heels, flimsy micro skirts, winking jewellery, low-cut clingfilm tops which riveted the eye to the firm high swell of silicone breasts. They stood with a studied provocative pose as if waiting for the paparazzi to arrive. Bysshe was the only girl here wearing a long skirt, the only girl not displaying a peep-show of naked flesh. She halted beside a lamppost and began salsa dancing. Salsa Dance #2 "hello Bysshe."

"Hello Lexus Mission."

Lexus Mission wore low-slung jeans with designer shorts showing above the waistband. A white t-shirt was drawn tight across his burgeoning chest. His beady magnified eyes shone as if smeared in a lubricant.

"how about a blowjob?" he said.

"Not in the mood," said Bysshe.

"that's a shame."

"Have you noticed that colours here are not affected by the lines that bind them?"

"u r a clever broad."

"That doesn't mean I don't enjoy the tickle of black lace against my inner thigh when I cross my legs."

"u r turning me on. Lol. i've got a big dick."

"But not the quantum secret."

"what the fuck is that?"

"The beauty of things so intricately small you can sense but not see them. Big belongs to the last century. You're an anachronism, Lexus."

"u r doing my head in."

"It's interesting how sexual rejection here has so little impact on self-esteem. At least if you're anything to go by, Lexus."

Hi guys," said Alyante Host who dropped down from the sky. "I've just been sky diving."

"I don't think you could ever break my brittle heart," said Bysshe.

"You on drugs?"

"Hi kids," said Professor Whitehead. He didn't look like a professor. He looked like a Scandinavian heroin addict.

"I only arrived today. There's not much here which might make you sad," said Bysshe. "Though there might be consequences. I haven't found that out yet."

"u r a nutjob."

"That may well be, Lexus. Have you noticed there are no old

people here? No fat people either. Everyone is twenty-two and selling sex. Anyway, I'm off now."

Bysshe Artaud flew up into the thin blue rinse of sky with a lunar lightness and hovered there. Bysshe Artaud was my newly-created avatar.

I'll explain why I created Bysshe Artaud but it might take a while. The other day I was driving my delivery van as I'd been doing for three months. It was my penultimate delivery. An address in Arundel. Picturesque place with its faux castle and second-hand bookstores and the swans preening about on the River Arun.

Delivering groceries in red plastic crates was as far removed from what I consider my native ground as I've ever been forced to venture. Every day I knew moments of belittlement, of humiliation. Any customer could knock me off the precarious perch of my self-esteem with a patronising gesture or remark. Most of us carry around the extravagant hope that the world can at least catch a glimpse of what we consider to be our true face. We can't help harbouring the desire that past achievements and former incarnations still reveal some glimpse of themselves on our person. That people might be able to read the history of a face and not just its live bulletins. Truth be told, I no longer looked at my face in mirrors. Except when I was shaving which, thankfully, I only have to do once every two weeks.

My life had folded itself into a concise hardened shape. It was as sharply and inexorably defined as a print in concrete. Sometimes, looking out at the world through my window, I was aware of possessing no point of contact. Nobody out there was waiting for me, nobody was out there looking forward to me.

There hasn't really been a second act in my life. I'm still wandering around in Act One. Often the opening refrain of a song buffeted me into reclaiming a ghost of myself. Time for me was running backwards, unfurling in multifaceted torn strips. The images I saw were often washed out and spectral as if consisting predominantly of reflected light. New experience for me had become simply the light shed on past experience by its retrieval from oblivion. I was most happy just idling away my time. I enjoyed observing the world continue without me. I have a talent for the things ghosts would excel at. I suspect this is the fate of all those who do not pass on their genetic material. Isn't that supposed to be nature's most urgent imperative? In that case I had cheated nature.

I was thinking about the man I had just delivered groceries to as I pulled up outside the house in Arundel. He had wanted me to see his true face. He was one hundred and two years old and fought in World War Two. In Africa and Italy. He didn't want to talk about Italy though. He wanted to talk about a girl. The girl he was betrothed to but who had betrayed him. When he returned from the war he discovered she had married someone else. But he remained faithful to her memory throughout his life. Never once even kissed another girl. I couldn't quite decide if this was admirable or absurd, vanity or virtue. He showed me a photograph of the two of them together. I could see nothing special about her. At face value she would be easy to replace. But, as I said, I was tired of being taken at face value myself so reproached myself for dismissing the love of his life on the same terms. He told me he had no surviving family. "I'm all alone in the world, with a ghost," he said. It occurred to me my situation wasn't very different except I wasn't quite sure as to the identity of my ghost.

As I was struggling with the three heavy plastic crates loaded with bagged groceries down the crazy-paved garden path an inrush of enlivening scent wanted to take me back in time. I was still puzzling where I had first known that scent when a woman in jeans and a green cardigan answered the door. The moment she saw me she rocked back on her heels and held onto the doorframe. Stricken with the kind of disbelief you only see on the faces of actors. I assumed she was an old fan and had recognised me, which rekindled all the humiliation I felt about my changed circumstances.

She eventually managed to say, "Nick. You don't recognise me, do you?"

I should have been flattered she still recognised me, whoever she was. Instead I found myself taken off guard and looking harder and harder at her. She was still shaking off her incredulity. My attempt at discovering her identity was like the early stages of sculpting a head in clay, the cutting away and kneading down of superfluous bulk to discover the face's essential shape.

"Linda," she said.

"Linda," I said. The miracle of personality suddenly flashed onto her face and with it a host of jumbled memories. I wanted to apologise, not only for not recognising her which had granted me an unwarranted advantage at her expense, but also for how much I had aged since our last meeting. As if this was a flaw in my character. As if I had now ruined her memories of me. No wonder we love art so much – the beauty that forever remains unaltered.

"I saw you the other night on TV," she said. "There was a documentary about the ten best New Romantic bands. You were number nine." She smiled and I saw more poignantly the person I had known. I possessed one photograph of Linda. We were sitting on a breakwater on Hove beach and she was wearing a pale blue jumper of mine and smiling the exact same smile she smiled now.

"We weren't a New Romantic band," I said. "We were better than that." I could still succumb to petulance when I felt my legacy was being belittled. I might have added, but for my innate distaste of ever coming across as pretentious, that we introduced too many dissident and dark elements into the harmonies of our music to ever fit comfortably into any genre of pop. "I've had a few dreams about you over the years," I said, to make amends for not recognising her.

"I still can't quite believe this. Come in."

I carried her shopping into the kitchen. There were three vases of irises on the large wooden kitchen table and a paperback novel.

"Did you ever make it up with David?" I could tell she wasn't interested in David. There was something else on her mind. She had picked up one of the plastic bags. She gripped it so tightly that some of the orange dye came off onto her hand.

"No. I've not even seen him since before I last saw you."

"I like some of his solo stuff."

This caused me a pang of irritation and jealousy. It surprised me how much fortitude the old grudge still possessed. I was piecing back together the brief time Linda and I had spent together. We met a year or so after the band had broken up and I was still a mess of moral indignation and self-pity. There was a weekend in Brighton we shared. She had driven me out of London. A memorable visit to Rodmell and Virginia Woolf's house and garden. I remembered the exalted idea of domestic harmony that house conveyed. *The Waves* was my favourite book. It moved me so deeply that it became a part of my mind.

"I'm sorry about suddenly disappearing," I said. "I was having a kind of breakdown. I went to Italy, to study sculpture. I stayed there two years. I decided everything on the spur of the moment. It was cowardly of me not to tell you."

She shrugged off my apology. I couldn't think of what to say next. I picked up the book on the table.

"*The Tree House* by Glenn Haybittle. Never heard of it," I said. "Any good?"

"It's okay. Not the best book I've read this year. I still can't believe this. I tried to get hold of you recently. You don't have any online presence at all, do you?"

"No. I tried Twitter, but I didn't get it. It struck me as a kind of supermarket where everyone turns themselves into merchandise."

"The only online site I like is Goodreads. I write a review there of all the novels I read. About three a week! I really enjoy it. I think I've become quite good at it."

"I haven't a clue what Goodreads is, but I always liked your mind," I said. This was true. She could convey herself with eloquent sincerity and enlivening warmth and often outwitted me when it was as if she had scooped up a handful of collected rainwater and allowed me to see myself reflected miniaturised in the palm of her hand.

"I can't believe this. There's actually something important I need to talk to you about."

"Oh?"

"How about if I make you dinner later? We can talk about it then."

I looked around, unconsciously perhaps searching for evidence of the presence of a husband. It surprised me that I was still in possession of some sexual vanity.

2

"Personal relationships are paramount in life. At their best they can confirm the highest ideals we have about human life. Relationships are how we learn about ourselves. How we evolve, both as individuals and communities. How we learn about the world around us. Relationships are the most accessible source of inspiration. They can bring us to our knees; they can move us close to heaven. Personal relationships are our sacred text, our scripture."

David said this in a recent interview. He was always more eloquent, more intelligent than I was. Except, like me, he was painfully shy (our shyness, a kind of social phobia, cemented the close bond between us). He hated giving interviews. Therefore, in the early days, every interview was done as a group. However, every time someone else answered a question, you could feel him bristle with embarrassment or irritation. The first sign of what a controlling person he was. Soon, he began taking over the interviews.

I met David at secondary school in Beckenham. My first week there I had two fights. The establishing of hierarchy at school begins quickly. Various factors play a part in establishing the class pecking order. How good you are at football matters, your haircut and what clothes you wear (the small liberties taken with the uniform; how you dress outside school); the music you like has little charge initially, but gradually begins to influence the vibe you give off, the quality of charisma you exude and it's a way to differentiate yourself, establish an individual identity.

To begin with, though, you're judged by how hard you are. I was immediately picked on because I looked like an easy target. I was very thin and my dark hair was girlishly dishevelled. However, years earlier, my mad alcoholic grandfather had given me boxing lessons after I had been picked on at primary school. I can still recall the imprisoning texture of the leather gloves on my hands. My grandfather enjoyed these sparring bouts - what man doesn't revel in the conferred authority of imparting knowledge? I hated them. Anyway, I didn't win either of my two fights, but I didn't lose them either. And, thankfully, they were to be the last two fights I ever had. I didn't join the hard gang, but neither was I in their sights as easy prey. Another advantage I had was that I was quick-witted. I was good at making people laugh. That makes you popular. People of all ages love to laugh. Soon, David and I were sitting at the back of class together. He didn't have to fight his own battles. The immunity to harm granted me by the hard boys was extended to him too. Neither of us were the slightest bit interested in lessons. I couldn't learn anything that didn't appeal to my imagination. I suspect David was the same.

David, like all of us, had a wide range of smiles. His delighted smile, still an eloquent definition of radiance in my memory, could make me feel a prize winner when I inspired it. This was one of the first things I learned about him.

Another early memory is the process by which us boys were chosen for rugby teams. The two captains were called upon to alternately select boys, one by one, for their team. I was always one of the last to be chosen; David was always the very last. The implication, of course, was that we were both virtually worthless. He didn't care, or so he said, but I always found this experience humiliating. In turn, he reprimanded me for always playing the joker. "I don't believe you're as happy and carefree inside as you make out." It was the first penetrating insight anyone had ever made about me. To be honest, it was the first time anyone had taken an informed interest in me. My mother and father were both remote figures in my childhood. Both went out of their way not to talk, not to listen.

Something David and I had in common was that neither of us had enjoyed our childhood, neither of us had felt protected or loved as children. We retreated into ourselves to find survival resources at a very early age. And, as a result, we were both too shy, too outwardly lonely, entirely miscast to relish the company of the rough kids in the rough area in which we grew up. We were loners. Both of our fathers were frustrated men with low-paying, physically tiring jobs. Both of our mothers struggled with the emotional challenges of motherhood. There was little laughter in either of our homes. In fact, I can remember virtually nothing about my life until the moment I met David. It's as if I've blocked it out.

We weren't yet very image-conscious. We were scruffy, and our hair was a little longer than the proscribed school length. This was the first look we later began to cultivate. My defining image of David during this early period of our friendship is of him standing with his hands deep in his trouser pockets, his arms pressed to his sides with a distant sulky look on his face.

I remember buying individual cigarettes in the local newsagents and smoking them together under the railway bridge. We both took to smoking. I liked holding something in my hand that could make me feel good. There was a philosophy in the act. Ironically, smoking for me has always imparted a life-affirming charge.

Soon we began hanging out together after school. We only truly came alive in each other's company. It was as if we had a secret pathway into each other's thoughts, as if we completed a circuit within each other. We never forget the first person who seems to understand us as we understand ourselves. Soon we could communicate with the faintest of gestures, with code words, with silence. No thought was complete until I had shared it with him. We believed we were creating a new reality together. David barely spoke to anyone else. In class he often blushed when a teacher singled him out. That he was so much at his ease with me made me feel privileged, singled out. We were famous for being inseparable. We never had enough time to say all the things we wanted to say to each other. Music soon became the outward expression of our bond. A kind of sequestered home we made for ourselves together. I remember for months I would say to him, what's your name? And he would reply, Virginia Plain. All our intimacy seemed to reside in that exchange. Music served as a shorthand to express our thrilling appreciation of each other's company which we never, in all the time we spent together, broached with any other kind of language.

At the same time David and I could both be overly sensitive and stubborn – quick to take exception, slow to make amends.

Listening to music together replaced our former habit of playing football in the street outside David's home. We did this every Friday night and only went out once to get some chips at the local fish and chip shop. David had a wholly unrealisable crush on a girl we often saw walking with her skinhead boyfriend. He was over six feet tall, very good looking with a scar on his cheek, an almost otherworldly figure with his shiny cherry-red Doctor Marten boots, his Sta-Prest trousers, braces, Harrington jacket and Ben Sherman checked shirt. The fear that combination of clothes evoked at this period of time was electrifying. You couldn't help, as a boy, being overawed. I used to rib David about how absurd, not to mention suicidal, was his desire to replace Scarface, but it was perhaps the first indication of how high David set his sights.

Two girls began to appear at a window we regularly walked past on our way to the fish and chip shop. Sometimes they danced there, other times they laughed and threw us provocative looks. It was the classic scenario: one was incredibly attractive and sexy, the other looked like a handmade rag doll. The grubby terraced house where they appeared at the window took on the air of an enchanted castle. It drew a sequestering circle of bewitchment around the moment. I felt as if a new neuronal circuit had been activated in my brain. It was like a Mediterranean coastal road, dipping and looping amidst olive groves and flowering vines. I learned in those days that it's the mind's apprehension of beauty which renews everything, which enables us to see the world for the first time again. Beauty is a private moment in the mind, which we then seek to communicate.

One evening, as we walked past, both girls lifted their tops to reveal their bras. The first sexual compliment I had ever received. My first love bite. Because eventually, by means of a messenger, a small sister, we discovered they both liked me and not David. David was once voted the best-looking man in the UK so that was quite a coup on my part. I felt bad for him at the time. But I also felt good about myself. When you discover someone is attracted to you it's like being pulled up on a stage out of the audience.

Not that this accolade had happy consequences. After this initial show of interest Lorraine, the girl in question, vanished. The house we walked past belonged to her friend's family. I couldn't wait for Fridays to arrive. But the enchanted house had been voided of all its magic. It became what it was, an unkempt non-descript terraced house with closed curtains. I learned that the gestures of girls were less explicable than those of boys. I also learned that girls could be generators of obsessive thoughts. The more elusive she became the more I thought about her. That was my pattern with girls for many years. I discovered with the help of the telephone directory that she lived in Balham. Balham was about five stops away on the train. I began to write her letters which she never answered. Several times I caught the train from Birbeck Station to Balham and walked back and forwards past her house. She had turned me into a stalker. Later, when we were famous, I had a few stalkers of my own. So did David, one of whom brandished a knife and asked him to cut her. She wanted him to leave an indelible mark on her body.

I never told David about these solitary odysseys to Balham. It was the first secret I kept from him. I should perhaps have felt guilty that I was putting Lorraine before him. I soon learned she frequented the most prestigious nightclub in the area, the Drum in Penge, where the two hardest boys in my class were occasional visitors. I learned this when excerpts from my letters were quoted at school. I later bumped into her friend who told me that if I ever wanted to get anywhere with girls I should stop being so nice. Truth be told, my distant and unemotional mother had made me feel rejected, so I never blamed any female for treating me as unlovable. It was what I warranted, expected and perhaps even sought. As if were any girl not to reject me it would reveal some fundamental lack of integrity in her. My mother later blamed the Cold War and the threat of nuclear extinction for all her shortcomings as a mother. She said the state of fear she lived in during that period froze over all other feelings. That was the explanation for her aversion to touching me or even being emotionally present when I needed reassurance. I didn't accept it as a valid excuse at the time, but now I'm older I understand better the crippling consequences of mental health issues.

I had an aunt who worked for Pye Records and every week she would send me two singles of my choice. Her bedroom, stacked wall to wall with record albums, was an Aladdin's cave to me as a teenager. I remember it was there I saw the gatefold sleeve of Jimi Hendrix's *Electric Ladyland*. My first visual sighting of bared female breasts. At every subsequent visit I covertly sought it out. I listened to pirate radio in bed, an early exciting transgression of household rules, and watched *Top of the Pops* every Thursday – both cherished pastimes through which I felt I was disassociating myself from my parents and the stifling obedience to convention that served as their creed. The opening music to *Top of the Pops* streamed through me the same wondrous anticipation I knew when I saw a virgin covering of snow outside my bedroom window as a tiny kid. Excitement experienced by children often has an undertow of guilt attached. My guilt was connected to the scantily clad female dancers on the show. My hot fascination with them I always sought to hide from my parents. It's strange how everything pivotal and deeply intimate you feel as a kid you feel compelled to hide from your parents, as if their horizons are much narrower than yours. Every week I would name to my aunt the two singles I most wanted. The arrival of these parcels was always the most anticipated event of the week. David would come round to my house and we would sit by my record player and share our rapture. I also remember my first tape recorder (partly paid for with Green Shield Stamps) and how exciting it was to record songs from the radio. My introduction to the wizardry of technology. I remember, aesthetically, we were much more interested in men than women (though I was smitten with Samantha in *Bewitched* and one particular member of the *Top of the Pops* dance troupe). Mostly, and without consciously realising it, I was looking for male role models. Marc Bolan partially answered that need for a while. I liked the greasepaint and glitter he wore around his eyes and his low-slung guitar. But it wasn't until that cultural watershed moment when David Bowie appeared on *Top of the Pops* doing 'Starman' that David and I truly found what we had been looking for. I remember my father was reading the paper in his armchair while this spellbinding three minutes of television took place. I thought the radiant magnitude of what I was watching would lift the roof off the house. It wasn't until half way through the song that he lowered his newspaper, looked at the TV screen and shook his head in scornful disbelief. I had been given an inheritance. That's what I felt. And that my father's generation had become suddenly obsolete.

The next day at school David and I looked at each other wide eyed. It was as if in three minutes we had been given a new language. David Bowie became our mirror. He had created an alternative world which articulated some of our most pressing wants. It was his physique as much as his androgyny that excited me. I was the thinnest boy at school and hated undressing in front of the other boys. My skeletal frame was a source of much mocking banter in the changing room. David Bowie made being thin cool. I began experimenting with my mother's makeup soon afterwards. One evening I dared myself to set foot outside the house with a painted face. I went for a ride on my bike. My father caught me when I returned home and hit me with his belt. The first and only time he hit me.

Thursdays were also exciting because new editions of the *NME* and *Melody Maker* appeared in the newsagents. (These replaced *Shoot*, the weekly football magazine, as my favourite reading matter.) I always derived satisfaction from buying these papers. It was one of my first adult transactions. They also introduced me to the joys of reading. Paul Morley was to become our favourite music journalist, the one we most wanted to love our music. Needless to say, he held us in contempt. At least until our fourth and final album *Scorched Earth*.

I think we were fourteen when David acquired a guitar. The initial plan was that I would be the singer in our band. The first time I sang in front of David I experienced agonies of self-doubt and expected him to laugh. I could only barely sing in tune and hated the sound of my voice. I was therefore less enthusiastic about the prospect of our imaginary band than David. At some point later David told me his uncle knew of someone selling a bass guitar for five quid. David persuaded me to buy it. I can't say bass players attracted me. Shadowy background figures who often, musically, contributed little more than the equivalent of a tapping foot. However, the first LP I ever owned was *Tamla Motown Chartbusters Volume Three* and even at a young age I was entranced, without quite realising it, by rhythm sections. Even before I could play the thing, I was determined to bring the bass into the foreground. An early sign perhaps that I was going to vie with David for centre stage. Therefore, in the early days, it was David on guitar and me on bass learning songs together. David usually sat cross-legged on the floor while I sat on the bed. I remember one of the first songs we struggled for weeks to master was 'Children of the Revolution' by T-Rex. *Well, you can bump and grind, it is good for your mind.*

One Saturday afternoon I saw three skinheads walking towards me. They had claret and blue scarves tied to their waist and were returning from a Crystal Palace home game at Selhurst Park, not far away. I immediately knew something bad was going to happen. A gust of polluted energy seemed to swirl over the street as if a plane had just flown really low overhead. It was simply my own apprehension. As I approached they spread out on the pavement so I couldn't pass. "What's that?" one of them said. He was referring to my bass inside its case. They were probably about my age. "Are you a queer?" another one said. Before I knew what was happening I was punched in the face and my guitar tugged out of my hand. They were laughing when they walked away with my bass, the most precious thing I owned. I tried unsuccessfully to fight back the tears. I was too ashamed to face David, to explain what happened, so I went home. When I did tell him, I turned it into a comic anecdote, which was often my way of dealing with hurt. Later that week my father brought home a new bass guitar for me. I forgave him all his shortcomings as a father for this gesture. I never forgot the kindness of that act. It came to represent my abiding feeling for my father.

In those days, at fourteen and fifteen years of age, I used to go to gigs. David's parents wouldn't allow him to accompany me so I always had to go alone. My first experience of being surrounded entirely by strangers, a condition I was to know well and enjoy much less when I reached middle-age. My parents raised no objections. By now they were turning a blind eye to all my adolescent static. My presence in the house was generally acknowledged with a defeated exasperated shaking of the head. The most memorable gigs I attended were The Who at the Oval cricket ground, Mott the Hoople at Croydon's Fairfield Halls and Roxy Music at the Crystal Palace Bowl. Every Sunday I would go to see bands at the Croydon Greyhound. I met my first girlfriend there. I was fifteen. Once a week Angie and I would go to the cinema together. I was delighted she shared David Bowie's wife's name. In the cinema she always put her hand in my lap and gently moved her fingers about. Underneath the pleasurable sensations I couldn't help feeling a bit confused. For one thing it surprised me that teasing an erection out of my body held any attraction for her. Especially inside a cinema where there was no possibility of it being anything but an end in itself. It also made me understand how shy I was. I didn't possess the audacity to reciprocate her bold generosity. When the lights came back on she kind of disowned all the foraging intimacy of her gesture. There was no acknowledgement of it in her eyes. We would act normal and talk about the film or superficial stuff. The memory of it would keep me awake at night. Of course, I couldn't wait for her to do it again. But it baffled me what she wanted in return. I felt my failure to understand showcased all my inept immaturity. However, the kisses we shared at the bus stop, the press of her warm body sequestered in all its female mysteries, were an introduction for me to the wonders that awaited me in the adult world. Afterwards, on my way home, I would marvel at her ability to root me so firmly in the moment, to feed so much vitality into my bloodstream, to galvanise me so magically into consciousness of her. I never told David about her. I didn't want him to feel jealous.

3

I was nervous when I arrived at Linda's. As a rule, I had always shrunk from any appointed task. Which made going out on stage a constant trauma for me. I'm incorrigibly lazy, especially when it comes to doing battle with my over-excitable nervous system. If I hadn't been a musician I would probably have been a tramp. Obsessively ritualistic, biting the hand that feeds, answering to no one but myself. I didn't want to go through with this encounter. I didn't want to go through any social encounter. I had put to bed my social self. My sexual self too. I had become a recluse. Every time, rarely, my phone rang I listened to it with the visceral dread induced by dentist drills or ambulance sirens. It always made me feel exposed and uneasy. I did not like unforeseen intrusions into my solitude.

I had revisited in as much detail as I could recall the time Linda and I had spent together. I met her a year or so after David's unforgivable act of betrayal. My self-esteem was at an all-time low. She was a selfless generous lover with an abundance of tenderness she could channel wholesale into her hands. Her body always gave off heat, as if she had run all the way to meet me. And she was a greedy soulful kisser. But our first attempt at making love didn't quite work out. I floundered at the moment of union. I couldn't find my way in, like someone trying to open a door with the wrong key. I couldn't find the animal in me. I've always struggled to come up with that possessive male thrust of ownership that men deploy to get right of way. I'm the same when driving. I rarely assert my will in an entitled manner. Anyway,

I was too shy to ask her to guide me in. And soon my body contracted in a cold jet-shower of embarrassment. Having failed once I was reluctant to try again. I had a horror of attempting in company anything I might prove inept at. I had always been scared of displaying ignorance. I once failed to open a bottle of champagne in company. I've never since tried to open another bottle. So Linda began to pleasure me. I sensed she was happy about this to some extent because she wasn't comfortable in her nakedness. She had some loose skin on her body which I sensed was a source of shame to her. Thus she seemed happy to put her hands on me so as to keep my hands off her. I remember there was a bounty of knowledgeable empathy in the touch of her fingers. As if she could feel every shiver of pleasure the caressing of her hands gifted to me on her own body. After weeks of carrying on like this, I managed to overcome my inhibitions and, in the missionary position and in the dark, we finally made love. I remember the night well because my cat gave birth to three kittens underneath my bed. I had experienced love largely as contests of will before Linda. There were no games with her. Perhaps because of an unaccounted ability she had to make her body proof of what she felt at source.

Linda poured me a glass of red wine and sat down opposite me at the kitchen table. The three vases of irises were still there but not the paperback novel. She told me I had a daughter. And before I could register the shock of this news she told me this daughter of mine had gone missing two weeks ago. She told me about the last two CCTV images of her the police had shown her. She described to me the grainy black and white images. How they made it seem Katie, her name, had walked off into a different universe the moment she exited the frame. How these images were now as if stamped on her retina, superimposed on everything she looked at, eclipsing every other pictorial detail she had of her daughter. As if she was now forever frozen in that final frame before she stepped out into the vast unknown.

"Her phone was found by the river. But I feel I would know if she wasn't alive. I don't feel she isn't alive."

Her lips twitched and then her face collapsed. She stared at me wide-eyed for a moment, her cheeks translucent with the first tears, then she brought her hands to her face and her body began to heave and rock from its core, and it was like she couldn't find enough air to breathe. It occurred to me that I had never come close to crying with such abandon. I moved over to her and felt awkward while I tried to comfort her. I remembered she had cried a lot. Gusting winds and downfalls of torrential rain were a big part of her emotional weather. Experience either hugged or harmed her. Her tears had always made me feel either helpless or indicted, as if there weren't sufficient stores of generosity in my nature. But I felt at home with Linda. I was never attracted to the kind of women who bring peace and quiet.

When she had composed herself she showed me photographs of Katie, most of them selfies downloaded onto social media accounts. My first impression was of the kind of ubiquitous young female face you see everywhere these days. Yearning with the aspiration to project beauty, independence and sex appeal. Initially, I was able to look at her face without any fatherly feeling. As if she was another female contender for the male sexual predator in me. The pleasure I felt in finding her attractive was quickly blemished with the black poisonous ink of taboo guilt. Then I began looking for myself in her features.

Later, to give me an idea of how contentious Katie could be, Linda let me read a letter she had sent her –

"Shall I tell you what a woman's most basic and compelling instinct is? It's to dissolve down into the fluid tides of her body. Our lives are a constant celebration of and battle against that coercive force. Of course it's terribly flattering to be turned into a bloodless icon and every woman will accept this honour as her right - but that's not how we want to spend our physical time - answering back to heavily annotated extracts from a sacred book. Women are messy and sporadic, cyclical and cruel. As a rule, we derive more gratification from our bodies than our minds. Women are biology at its most intractable and ruthless."

"She's certainly got a creative mind," I said. I had felt a rush of pride while reading her words. I liked her intelligence, even though I can't quite say I understood it. My first ever experience of fatherly pride. My daughter's ideas made me think of Linda's wholehearted tears earlier and, in turn, the ability of women to surrender themselves with more abandon to the tides of the body than men. At times, taking myself as a model for my sex, I couldn't help thinking of women as an upgraded version of men.

"A lot of the time she says things she doesn't mean," said Linda. "It's difficult getting on with anyone like that."

"Did you tell her about me?"

"A couple of years ago. We sat down together and watched YouTube videos of Orfée. She was dismissive of your music. She called it pretentious pop music. She wasn't very flattering about you either. She said you were just another David Bowie clone. But I think we watched every single piece of footage of you there is online. A few weeks later she posted one of the videos with the caption "my dad". It got loads of likes and OMGs and a couple of her friends commented on how beautiful you were."

Linda then told me Katie had struggled through lengthy periods of eating disorders, and a phase of cutting her legs and arms. That she had been on and off medication for her violent mood swings. She told me home life had been an unceasing civil war. That Katie had blamed her for everything she didn't like about her own life and for everything she didn't like about the world.

"The Tory government, that was my fault, even though I didn't vote for them. Racism was my fault because I have no ethnic minority friends. Global warming, that was my fault, too. Every night at dinner she would describe to me catastrophes that will happen if the planet continues warming at its present rate. She took an angry delight in describing these projected calamities and laid them out like evidence in a courtroom, as if I was in the dock. She would attack me for how much washing I do, how much food I waste, for eating meat and dairy produce, for driving my car instead of walking. For her our generation is single-handedly responsible for desecrating the planet. Like we've treated the planet as a festival site. Her stepfather, when he was alive, didn't help matters. He was a reactionary Tory. The shameful *Daily Mail* was his scripture."

I expressed my sympathy at the death of her husband.

"He loathed you. It disgusted him that you wore makeup. And especially that you were wearing makeup when we made love. I couldn't stop myself from telling him that. Katie, on the other hand, loved it that she had been conceived with the help of a man wearing eyeliner and ivory foundation."

This made me laugh.

"You and Katie would get on well, you know. My husband, though, you would have loathed back. He had hit me the night before he died. A stinging slap which left a mark. He was drunk and accused me of flirting with a dinner guest. It wasn't the first time. I was actually full of hatred for him the moment before he died. He was hit by a bus. A bee was buzzing around his head as we walked down the road. He began to panic and swat madly at the air. I remember thinking what a pathetic cowardly man he was. He lost his sense of bearings and tripped on the edge of the pavement and fell into the road just as a bus was approaching. I can still hear the noise of the impact. I've grown to no longer hate him, but I must have been out of my mind when I married him. Of course, I was pregnant then and thinking almost entirely in practical terms. But he was a scathing and grotesque misrepresentation of everything I aspired to. And it's soul-destroying to be so horribly misrepresented every day of your life. Often, when he was angry, he used to throw the book I was reading across the room. I think he sensed I could only find in books many of the things I needed from a man. He made Katie's life difficult too. She says he abused her. When she was fourteen. He placed her hand on his erection over his trousers. Knowing him, I expect he tortured himself afterwards. But it would have made him dislike her. And me too. Which became more than evident. Whenever we went abroad he would insist upon ham rolls for lunch and a steak for dinner. That's the kind of man he was."

The story of her husband's death took me back to my own childhood. Two girls lived at the back of our garden and they were my playmates. Rose was my age and the first love of my life. Martha, her sister, was older and it was she who decided what games we played, she who instigated the wickedness. Soon we were playing nurses. Martha told Rose she had to make my thingy feel better. On my bedroom floor my shorts were pulled down and Rose sheepishly touched my most secret part. In the following days she grew bolder and at the age of eight I had my first orgasm, a watered-down facsimile of the adult cocktail version but immensely pleasurable all the same. We knew we were doing something taboo. But we were safe from adult censorship. It was always much more difficult to find my mother than to hide from her. Martha died the day after we had played one of these games. She was pretending to be a ballerina on a kerb, toppled and was hit by a lorry. At the funeral me and Rose looked at each other in the midst of all the adult grief. The guilty knowledge of our games was in the look we gave each other. It was like we were the only people there who knew why Martha had died. I think we both wondered why we hadn't died too.

"In the months before she disappeared Katie stopped going out. She was always online. I think she got in with some like-minded people. Eco warriors or whatever they call themselves. From what I can gather she met them in a virtual world called Second Life. Have you heard of it?"

4

I hadn't consciously chosen a female avatar to be my envoy in this virtual world. She had gradually evolved while I was editing the appearance of my original male avatar. Somewhere along the line Bysshe had begun to take on a female aura. As if she was making informed demands of me. She seemed more grounded in herself when I gave her breasts.

To begin with I experienced difficulty in getting Bysshe to follow my commands. Often she faltered jauntily into partitions or synthetic shrubbery and got herself trapped. She had a talent for disappearing into her performances, something most of us are good at when arguing with the politics of a place. Once she had inadvertently walked into someone's house and been fired at by a man with a shotgun. The animation was quite impressive – a bolt of electricity seemed to rocket through his upper body every time he pulled the trigger. About fifteen rounds went off. There was a hollow popping noise inside my headphones. The alarm I had felt was only partly virtual. Real chemicals had been released into my bloodstream. I still didn't know then it was impossible to die in Second Life.

I spent an hour teleporting Bysshe to a succession of what I was informed were popular places – clubs and casinos, shopping malls and beaches - where I eavesdropped on what were mostly inane conversations. The gaze of all the avatars is manically intent, almost chemically heightened. Every figure gazes around, up at the sky, down at the ground with a kind of dumbstruck delighted awe.

In a nightclub a few avatars were dancing to soulless Euro disco music.

"Hello," said Jungi Masukami. He had circular eyes the colour of frozen spinach.

"Hi," said Bysshe. I clicked on my inventory and selected a model pose for her to adopt. She stood with one hand on her hip and her head inclined to one side in a sultry fashion. She looked like she wanted to spit at Jungi Masukami.

"China English learn happy you?"

"You had better start kissing some booty," said Estrella Lehman who was dressed in fetish gear.

"Thank you," said Jungi.

I clicked on Showcases - there was Princeton University, the Museum of Philosophy, Rome, the Planetarium Dome. All these places were empty. I tried Events. There was a women's bible study group, a rave, an art exhibition. I teleported Bysshe to the latter.

The canvases on the walls in the Rainbow Arcade Gallery were like charity Christmas cards. They all had price tags. The cynic in me was wondering if this virtual world wasn't some kind of elaborate rehab centre for all those whose efforts at love and fame and creativity had met with rejection in the real world.

Bysshe sidled up to a bohemian type with a bandana sitting in the lotus position on a rug. He was attended by a young female acolyte. He was the only avatar I had encountered so far who looked older than twenty-one. You could decide what level of wrinkling you wanted. Everyone typed in 0%.

"You look like you might have gathered some wisdom in your travels," said Bysshe demurely.

"Thank u."

"And these are your paintings?"

"Yes. Right click to buy anything you like."

I was getting disheartened. How could any daughter of mine find nightly nourishment amongst all this gibberish? What did she do in here? It was hard to believe there was anything in this world that might bring one closer to things one didn't know about oneself.

I decided I would give it another hour. Bysshe joined a dole queue on a tropical island. Here she was paid $3 for every ten minutes she remained on her poseball. The sun was rising and a muted red blush seeped up into the black sky and its grid of unblinking satellites. For a moment it looked like Bysshe was bathing in the afterglow of the moment of creation. The avatar in front of her in the queue had a guitar and, so his script informed me, was playing Sabbath riff 1. I could hear it struggling to attain resonance in my speakers. There wasn't much conversation in the line so I decided it was up to Bysshe to break some ice.

Bysshe cupped her hands around her mouth, threw back her head and shouted:

"Don't you think sex is often like finishing a good book? Afterwards you're not quite sure if something wonderful has just become a part of your life or if something wonderful has just departed from your life."

All the avatars in line fidgeted, one sneezed, but no one replied.

I right-clicked on the profile of the avatar behind Bysshe. She was dressed in black, vain of her sophistication, and holding a small briefcase as protectively as women hold small children. Her name was Enigma Jewell. Her profile told me she was a member of the Stonegate Castle and that she had slaves, but that they weren't for sale.

"Would you like to make me one of your slaves, Enigma?" asked Bysshe.

There was no reply. Sabbath riff 1 started up again. And then Enigma Jewell dematerialised. I had the suspicion Bysshe had driven her away. Bysshe often had this effect on her fellow avatars. Most people gave the impression of being fully committed to their virtual selves; poor Bysshe, on the other hand, was saddled with an overflow of my own cynicism which aroused mistrust.

There was now the sound of a red-alert siren coming from my speakers. Balls of puffy green smoke began rolling across the screen. You could sense an attack of some kind was imminent.

"Griefers," said Zaine Hastings.

"XXX Wicker Graves tried to give me a virus," said Otti Volmar.

A message appeared on my screen asking if I wanted to accept a hub called b:places from XXXWicker Graves. I declined. Bysshe appeared much more restless, as did all her fellow welfare claimants. The burgeoning sunrise had now been overlaid by a wallpaper of malevolent cuddly toys. They floated across the sky with an oddly military intent. The tropical island suddenly darkened. All visuals then disappeared for a moment. The next time I saw Bysshe, her limbs were flaying about and she appeared to be tumbling down from some great height. She landed with a silent splash at the bottom of an ocean. She was surrounded by a heap of bewildered avatars, all gingerly getting back on their feet. Whoever had pulled off that little stunt was undoubtedly feeling very pleased with themselves now.

Bysshe had blagged $6 from the welfare state so I decided to take her shopping, see what I could buy for six dollars. I was growing increasingly critical of her appearance. I couldn't help noticing that most of the female avatars were more beautiful and much more stylishly dressed. Once upon a time I loved shopping for clothes, traipsing around London's streets with David - Camden Market, Kensington High Street, the King's Road. Our made-up faces, women's earrings and dyed hair attracting interest and hostility in equal measure. We were gullible consumers, half-believing a more glamorous life was something that first had to be rung up on a till. It's hard for me now to fully appreciate how much renewed hope in the future a new article of clothing can feed into your bloodstream. But I remember the day in Covent Garden we discovered jazz shoes, elegantly androgynous, and solved the dilemma of our everyday footwear. Memories of shopping with David are among those that make me miss him the most. The relief in our tired legs at the end of the day when we sat down together in a café, our eyeliner a little smudged, and lit a cigarette and ordered a coffee. Nowadays my skin prickles with self-consciousness in shops, except those which don't contain anything I can't afford. That, I suppose, limits my shopper comfort zone to newsagents. I don't feel particularly pressurised or self-conscious in newsagents. There are no predatory shop assistants feigning benevolence in newsagents. This was also the case in all Second Life shops. You just browse and right-click on anything which takes your fancy and the price appears and the option of buying or cancelling. The trouble was Bysshe couldn't afford a single thing in the shop in which she now found herself. Red Designer Bling dress was $499; Pearl "as Nature Intended" Skin $2,000; Retro Polka Dot underwear $175. There was also property. $600 a week for a house in a PG sim with 300 prims in a well-lit neighbourhood with lots of trees providing shade from the sun. You're not going to earn that kind of money standing in the welfare line. Bysshe marched up to a fellow shopper.

"How can you afford to buy this stuff?"

"I make clothes and have five shops in SL where I sell them. But you can also use a credit card," said Arana Persia.

"Real money?"

"You get about 200 linden dollars for one US dollar. Otherwise why don't you try one of the free places? They've got loads of things and some of them are quite cool. I'll give you a landmark. And a gift. Hang on."

A message popped up on my screen. Arana Persia has given you an item called White Beaded Victorian Wedding Dress.

"I copied it from a real life dress in a museum. Try it on."

With some help from me, Bysshe stripped naked in the middle of the shopfloor and struggled into the white wedding dress. There was a bit of it missing for a while so that she had a bare buttock exposed.

"Stunning," Bysshe fibbed. "I could step into a Pre-Raphaelite painting holding this pose and no one would notice I was an illegal immigrant. I'm never going to take it off."

"Normally it would cost $900."

"I wish I could give you something in return."

"Just wear it and every time someone asks where you got it drop my notecard into their inventory."

"Okay."

"Can I ask you something?"

"Sure."

"Are you a male or a female?"

This question took me back in time. More than once, me and David had been stopped in the street and asked this same question, sometimes with genuine confusion, other times with hostile scorn. Then, it had never bothered me. Now it did. I was suddenly made to feel insecure on Bysshe's behalf. Then it occurred to me this person might be referring to me personally. She had been kind to me and I didn't want to deceive her.

"I thought I was female," Bysshe said.

"LOL. Stay still. I'm going to take a closer look."

I was slightly unnerved, as if Arana Persia was peering in at me through some crack in the door.

"Will you do as I say?" said Arana.

"Why not? How come everyone else looks so elegant?"

"They buy designer clothes. Go to expensive hair salons. You've just got some of the free stuff, right?"

"Yep."

"I can make you look better. Right click and then click on Appearance."

I did what she told me.

"Okay. You need a complete makeover. Quite a bit of surgery. Breast implants, nose surgery, face laser resurfacing, liposuction. First of all, let's make your neck thinner."

I followed her instructions for the next five minutes. Bysshe, still vertical, helpfully splayed out her legs and arms while surgery was carried out on her. I watched her cheekbones become chiselled, her lips fill out, her eyes assume a more exotic almond shape, her neck lengthen, her cleavage expand, her belly and thighs deflate, her legs elongate, her fingers taper elegantly. It was a bewitching pantomime of what most of us would like to do in front of a mirror.

"What do you think?"

"I look like all my prayers have been answered," said Bysshe.

I was reminded of when I first started wearing makeup. How easy it soon became to make my face look exactly how I wanted it to look. My face in the mirror often startled me with its uncanny faithful depiction of what I felt to be my true self. Even though, secretly, I knew it was a con trick. David, in later interviews, told the press we were thrown out of school for wearing makeup. This was another of his lies. Had we worn makeup to school we would have been beaten to a pulp and then suspended. Our only rebellious deviation from the uniform was wearing black loon pants and sometimes a coloured shirt. We began wearing makeup after we left school. It was however true that we wore it every day, all day.

Bysshe befriended Arana Persia. On the whole people are commendably kind and generous in Second Life. Certainly much more so than in the real world. I can't imagine asking someone for advice in Harrods and the next thing you know they've made you a present of a $900 Victorian wedding dress.

I said goodbye to Arana and teleported Bysshe to the free store and picked up some new outfits. I did some more editing on Bysshe's appearance. I changed the depth of her lip cleft and the angle of her chin; I made her jaw less pointed, gave her a more upturned nose and filled out her upper cheeks a little. She looked a little less bulimic now. I then tried on various things I had got from the store and finally settled on a Gothic skin with red lips, a black cherry bra and panties and her new white wedding dress. I had never seen her look so beautiful.

I thought I'd now seek out some culture. Shakespeare brought up two results from the search engine: The Globe Theatre and

Shakespeare & Co Book Store in Paris. I teleported Bysshe to the Globe. She walked down the centre aisle towards the stage where a man was sitting on a stool. He wore a top hat, a waistcoat and a vampire cape. His eyes were heavily circled with eyeliner. I rather liked the look of him. Bysshe might possibly have fancied him. She seemed more aquiver than usual, her body language slightly shyer. He was called Primo Balhaus.

"Hi Babe," said Bysshe, ambling towards him in her wedding dress. "Rehearsing for a big moment?"

"Hello Bysshe. About to give a poetry reading actually."

"Are you nervous?"

"A bit because it's the first time I'll be going out on music stream."

Bysshe succumbed to a moment's tenderness for Primo.

"Why don't you hang around? It starts in five minutes," he said.

"Can I hear one of your poems now?"

"Sure. How about Miranda on Methadone?"

"Cool."

Author reads: Miranda is sitting on a stone.

Author reads: Miranda is on methadone.

Author reads: It is no longer the sea she hears.

Author reads: Neither can she see any end to her fears.

Author reads: Miranda is on methadone. (The End)

"If I could applaud I would," said Bysshe.

I could feel a computerised affection begin to grow between the two heartless and bloodless emissaries on my screen. I too partook in it to some extent. It was like the vicarious warmth you feel for a character in a film who has endeared him or herself to you.

Avatars of a bohemian and intellectual appearance had begun to show up and were milling about in the aisles of the theatre. Bysshe took a seat in the lower stalls. The lights dimmed and for a few minutes I listened to the real voice of Primo reading his poems, a pleasing southern American drawl. Bysshe befriended

Primo before I took her back out into the open air. She had made two new friends today and I was proud of her.

I noticed a lone female avatar standing by the side of the river. Bysshe stomped over to her.

"Pensive?" said Bysshe.

"Oh hi."

"You look a bit sad," ventured Bysshe.

"You're on the money there. You a mind reader?" asked Kirsty Rivers.

"I could read your palms if you want."

"LOL. You don't have to."

"Oh?"

"I've just found out my husband is cheating on me."

"Real life?"

"No. In here. With a guy called Bud Lemon. I've hired a private investigator to set up a trap. I'm waiting for him to get back to me now."

"A real private investigator?"

"No. Avatar."

My eyes lit up. For the first time the idea of trying to find my daughter in this world occurred to me. There were apparently 70,211 people online here tonight. In other words, if my daughter was here, it would be like trying to find her inside Old Trafford on a Champions League night. I then noticed that over one million two hundred thousand people had been online in the past sixty days which, somewhat less heartening, would be akin to trying to track down Katie in Finland or Moldavia.

"If he's cheating on me with this Bud guy I'm going to divorce him."

"For having sex in here?"

"It's gross. And he's having sex with another man for chrissake."

"I've never had sex in here. Isn't it pretty harmless?"

"No. It's gross."

"And you'll divorce him in real life."

"Sure will. I've made up my mind."

"How long have you been married?"

"Twelve years."

"Surely if you're married you can just burst in on your husband while he's at his pc having virtual sex?"

"He's in his study and locks the door."

"So you're both in the same house and yet the only way to catch him in the act is to hire a virtual private detective?"

"Crazy isn't it?"

One thing I was learning here. It's true what they say. Most people, secretly, are insane.

"What's the name of this private investigator?"

"Tobias Hives. Actually, he's calling me now. My husband is with this Bud guy in a place called the BDSM Fetish Club. What does that stand for?"

"BDSM? Not sure. Bondage and dominance are in there though," said Bysshe softly. Unlike me she succumbed to no urge to giggle.

"OMG."

"Sorry."

"It's not your fault. Thanks for listening."

The moment poor Kirsty vanished, I typed Tobias Hives into the search engine. The snapshot of him showed a dandy with a cane, pince-nez and floppy dark hair over his eyes. Private investigator. Very discreet. Reasonable rates. His offices, I read, were in Stigma City. I sent a friend request to Kirsty Rivers in case I needed more info and then teleported Bysshe to Stigma City.

5

David and I both left school at sixteen as academic failures. I didn't bother writing a single word on any of my O-level papers except my name. It was act of rebellion against my mother who took far more interest in my academic progress than in any other aspect of my life. My mother and I constantly fought in a battle to exhaust each other's energies, to subdue each other into a temporary submission. She had to endure excessive measures of hostility from me. My parents had become oppressive strangers to me. I couldn't talk to either of them without arguing. And I derived no sense of self-worth from their company. Just the opposite. We were a family who touched each other only with extreme reluctance, with a slight shiver of repulsion even. I remember when the miners were on strike and there were power cuts virtually every day. We had to do everything by candlelight and it was the first time I felt some authenticity enter my parents' home. As if all the shadows my parents sought so exhaustively to conceal were suddenly prominent and alive. When the lights came back on, I knew I had to get out of that house as soon as possible. At the end of the day openly fighting with your parents is as pointless as trying to get a consolation goal when you're five-nil down with only ten minutes of the game left.

So I left home at sixteen and moved into a squat in Beckenham, a large neglected three-story house with a vast overgrown garden. I lived on the top floor with a boy who modelled himself on Che Guevara, his German girlfriend who did most things in her sex-shop underwear and a lanky long-haired boy called Kevin who was sadistic. He liked to instigate mock fights during which he took pleasure in physically causing me pain. My housemates were all older than me and smoked dope virtually all day. Together with David I tried virtually every chemical substance that year. Neither of us took to cannabis or any other drug. Music and wearing makeup was our drug. How we achieved a sense of exaltation.

A drug dealer lived on the ground floor and there were several police raids on the house. I remember there was a giant Victorian wardrobe in my room that, when we tried to move it, got lodged in the doorway. I thus knocked out the back, covered it in papier-mâché and painted it black and silver so it looked like a kind of cave you had to walk through to enter my bedroom. The police therefore were highly suspicious of my room. It was comical to watch them clamber into the wardrobe which wobbled when stepped into, and then come out the other side.

I got a job in a record shop in Oxford Street. I was able to steal half a dozen albums every week. I had no scruples about stealing. At an early age I began stealing money from my mother's purse. It became a kind of unthinking habit, like eating biscuits. I also stole books from Foyles in Charing Cross Road. Thinking about it now I'm amazed at my audacity, my arrogant sense of entitlement. I don't recognise this thief as a facet of who I am. I expect though all criminals say something similar about the relationship they have with their crimes.

On the platform at Beckenham Junction station every morning I met Alan who had been in our class at school and now worked for an insurance firm in Blackfriars. We had barely ever spoken at school because he always sat in the front row of classes and was studious. I told him about our ambition to form a band and he said he wanted to join, even though he couldn't play any instrument. I suggested he learned keyboards. Pete, who became our drummer, worked with me in the record shop.

We began using my room as a rehearsal space. Pete's elemental drum kit became a permanent fixture in my bedroom.

This was 1976 and punk was about to explode. I had already begun dyeing my hair. It was first jet black with blue streaks; then *Man Who Fell to Earth* orange. David's hair was now long and bleached white. The first time I saw him with bleached hair and eye-liner I was startled by how beautiful he was. The rather non-descript self-effacing boy he had been at school was transfigured, as if a wand had been waved over him. He looked like Brigitte Bardot at her most beautiful. We used to get our hair done in a salon in Kensington. Always an exciting expedition. I associate those trips to the hair salon with double-decker red buses. David and I sitting side by side upstairs, wearing makeup, smoking cigarettes. Whenever, often, the bus got stuck in traffic it would shudder like a fat animal that's just been shot by a tranquilliser dart. And I remember how our fellow passengers seemed in their wary insulation like a congregation of creatures of a different species with whom momentarily we were forced to share the same habitat. We were obnoxiously convinced of pioneering some elite cult in those days. I feel some nostalgia for the old red buses of the past that you could hop on and off at will. Nowadays the only way out of a bus is a door you can't open with your own hands. How smugly proud we are of our new-found freedoms in the West – always bragging about them and trying to export them further afield – and yet every year some sly little technological theft of our autonomy is surreptitiously introduced into everyday life. I mean, what better definition of prison is there than an enclosed space whose door you can't open with your own hands?

Cinema played a big formative part in our lives during this time. The Scala in King's Cross, the Ritzy in Brixton, the Gate at Notting Hill. We loved Cocteau's films, Fellini, Visconti and almost everything with Dirk Bogarde in it. Our love of these films became an important part of how we liked to see ourselves, which included a precocious and precarious aspiration to pass as intellectuals. To be honest, I was often impatient for the film to end because the moment I most relished was stepping back out into the world outside which always seemed newly minted after sitting in the dark for so long. At those moments I felt like a struck tuning fork vibrating with its one clear ringing note. We also discovered Erik Satie at this time. David began learning piano and spent a year trying to compose a song that sounded like Gymnopedies which eventually found form in 'The Folded Map' on *The Touch of Ghosts* album.

The real revelation of this period was just how deeply I fell in love with the bass guitar. I was still officially the band's singer and frontman at this point. I think the others were too kind to tell me how bland my voice was. But, deep down, I knew I would never acquire the confidence to step out onto a stage and sing. Which just left me with the bass. And, initially, I could find no glamour in being a bass guitarist. We were far more concerned with how we looked than how we sounded early on. But soon my bass became both my most inspiring ally and my most worthy opponent. Not dissimilar in fact to the bond I shared with David. I quickly abandoned the plectrum and began playing with my fingers. David was besotted with the New York Dolls at this time. I saw little merit in them. They were little more than a novelty band to me. And thoroughly boring as musicians. Arguably they were the prototype for punk – and, musically, punk too left me cold though I enjoyed its aesthetic. I was far more ambitious in terms of musicianship. The bass line on Lou Reed's 'Walk on the Wild Side' was an early revelation. It showed me the bass could have a narrative voice; that it wasn't there merely to furnish backdrop. This idea was still more eloquently articulated by Percy Jones' bass playing on Brian Eno's *Another Green World*. I spent hours trying unsuccessfully to mimic Percy Jones. Soon, while David was still obsessed with the New York Dolls, Pete and I, jumping way ahead of ourselves, were listening to Stanley Clarke and Billy Cobham. The harmonics, the sliding notes, the popping and slapping for which I became relatively well-known were mostly stolen from Percy Jones and Stanley Clarke. If you're learning any craft my advice would always be to emulate and aspire to a master. Sure, you're placing an obstacle field in your path, but what is happiness after all if not the over-coming of obstacles?

Late in the year Alan's brother offered us a gig at his wedding. We still had no material of our own. We were playing covers – I remember Bowie's 'Moonage Daydream' (without of course Mick Ronson's inspired electrifying guitar solo), the New York Dolls' 'Jet Boy', the Velvet Underground's 'Sweet Jane' and T Rex's 'Metal Guru' among others. At rehearsals I always made sure my voice could barely be heard over the instruments. The closer the gig got the more power it acquired to terrify me, until, in my head, it accumulated much of the menace of life-threatening surgery. It closed off to me every horizon. I couldn't see through to the other side. The most daring thing I had done up to that point was, when I was about fourteen, to enter a porn shop near Piccadilly Circus and somehow find the confidence to pick up a magazine and take it to the counter. I remember it told a kind of Lady Chatterley story: a posh woman in tweed and jodhpurs seduced by a farmhand. The abiding emotion it gave me was a sense of inadequacy about the size of my own equipment. Anyway, I had to own up that I would not be able to sing in public. And that's when David became the frontman. It surprised us that he knew all the lyrics to the songs we planned performing. As if he had known all along I would bottle out when the moment of truth arrived. No real mystery there as he knew me almost as well as I knew myself. By now, like a married couple, we could both detect every false note in the other's voice. I remember little about that gig except how sick with nerves I was. People say performing in front of people the first time is like stripping in front of a lover for the first time. But it's much more terrifying than that. At least a lover has an inclination to overlook anything unseemly. It's more like stripping naked in a high street shop window.

David's singing voice surprised me. In the early days it was gravelly and rasping, with Bowie cockney intonations and an overwrought breathlessness that made him sound like someone whose ability couldn't carry the weight of his ambition. To be honest, I suspected we would have to find a new singer. Alan could barely play more than five chords on his electric piano and there was some thought we might have to find a new keyboards player too. He seemed to have no natural aptitude for the piano at all. We still didn't have a name for the band. We had recently seen Cocteau's Orpheus trilogy for about the sixth time so David suggested the name Orfée. We thought we would change the name at some point but never did. In my experience, it's difficult to change any established name. Names quickly accrue significance and convey identity; they grow roots. I sometimes wonder how women feel when they marry. The abrupt discarding of the name by which they have always known themselves must be hugely disorientating. Like becoming an imposter overnight.

Soon the four of us began spending all our spare time together. The time had arrived to start writing our own songs and establish a musical identity. Alan bought a Moog synth and this added a new dimension to our sound. Though he was never to master the piano he possessed a natural gift when it came to mining the possibilities of synthesisers and sequencers. We were still struggling to learn our instruments together. It seemed to take an age to make tangible progress. I thought David would begin revealing more about himself in his lyrics, but the opposite was true. Every new song was like a new mask. I didn't like his lyrics in those days. They were pretentious. As a band we were noisy. Not much else.

I had another girlfriend by now. She was called Joanne. She was blonde and very beautiful. A lovely girl. We never though went much further than kissing. I was still a virgin. She gave me a kitten for my birthday. Ariel was white with black thumbprints. Considering how young I was I took good care of her. (It was one of her kittens, Geronima, that gave birth to another generation of kittens under my bed the night Katie was probably conceived.) I took better care of Ariel than I took of

Joanne. I finished with her after a couple of months without really knowing why. Sometimes I find myself wishing that we could make amends later in life to the people we treated harshly. It was through her that I began to realise how much potential there was for jealousy between David and me. I didn't like him talking to Joanne. He didn't like my relationship with her. He made me feel I was betraying the band by spending any time at all with her. He was very possessive. Perhaps that's why I ended things with her.

The next girl in my life was called Indira. She was a few years older than me, a beautiful wafer-thin Indian girl. She came home with me the night we met, and I lost my virginity with Brian Eno's *Discreet Music* playing in the background. I was far too focused on not appearing inept to derive much pleasure from the experience. We went on seeing each other for a couple of weeks. I remember she wore skimpy cotton knickers with some kind of faded pattern on them and a discoloured label poking out of the waistband at the back. The kind of knickers that have gone through the wash too many times. And a bra of a different and incongruous colour. I could tell she wouldn't think to wear anything special to have sex in, no favourite silk or lace ensemble, as if the act of love demanded no more protocol than a trip to the supermarket or cleaning the bathroom. I was a young boy. I still lived predominantly in my imagination and I needed girls to establish a creative existence there. Throughout my adolescence women to me had been represented by the nymphs in Waterhouse paintings. Those girlish maidens trembling with provocative passivity. The girls in those paintings were what I looked forward to. They filled my nights with poeticised erotic speculation. Quite simply, they appealed to my imagination. It's probable that male fantasies don't evolve to any great extent. We men need to dress desire up. We are sustained by mirages. That can be the trouble with us. Half the time we think reality is nothing but an extension of our own imagination. I sometimes suspect there's less blood, more imagination, in the feelings of men than there are in those of women. Indira showed me that sex ought to be a more naked act. A revelation I wasn't then primed to embrace.

The main problem with Indira was her high opinion of me. I couldn't take it seriously. As I've said, my mother and her aversion to any feeling which had a swell and a momentum to it had instilled in me a deep-rooted conviction that I was unlovable. Any girl who contradicted this feeling had no authority for me. I began to experience Indira as suffocating, grasping, melodramatic. Thus I had little inclination to go on seeing her. Except often she would be sitting on my doorstep at night when I returned home. As is the case with Joanne, I wish now I could make amends to Indira. I was wrong to scorn her belief in me. I realise now it was heartfelt.

At work one day in the record shop we had the radio on. Capital radio. And they were offering a council flat to the first five listeners to get through on the phone line. Pete convinced me to call. I did and the next thing I knew the radio was broadcasting my voice on air. I had won a council flat in Greenwich. When I say won I don't mean they gave it to me free of charge. I had to pay rent, but I could move in almost immediately. Thus it was that David, Pete and I moved into the top floor flat of a council block overlooking the river. The estate, divided up into precincts of geometric blocks, was the locus of so many crimes there was not a square inch of its reinforced concrete which would refuse to yield up forensic evidence. Lawns of broken glass and blanched junk food wrapping connected one phallic structure to another, all of which bore the names of English poets. We lived in Shelley block, our windows faced Wordsworth block.

I was listening to lots of bass-heavy roots reggae and dub at this time. And Pete was constantly pounding away at his drum kit. Not ideal for ingratiating ourselves to our neighbours. And soon they were complaining about the noise. In particular one white-vested shaven-headed man who lived below us. One time he was visible through the frosted glass of the front door shouting obscenities at us and wielding a pick-axe. The three of us hid. We found a rehearsal studio nearby – Kate Bush also used it, but we never saw her. The area we now lived in was more dangerous than Beckenham. Young males roamed around the littered streets in packs, making a raucous song and dance of their masculinity. I was mugged at knife point by four black guys one night. I remember one of them seemed ashamed of what he was doing, especially when I told them I was an impoverished musician. I can still clearly see his face, a kind face. At the time it saddened me that black guys saw me as a target and not an ally. In my mind, my made-up face and coloured hair separated me from the ruling establishment and all its racist associations. I was no less an outcast than they were. There should, I felt, have been solidarity. I was also punched in the face by two white guys in the middle of the afternoon. I was wearing Clinique Black Honey lipstick that day. I tried to make believe this didn't bother me so much because I felt superior to these small-minded petty criminals. But being hit in the face is an incredibly intimate and emotive experience. Few experiences rival it for the intensity of its invasive charge. It takes time to accommodate the personalised shock of it. If I multiply the harrowing shock of that experience by about a thousand I think I might be close to understanding what it must feel like to be raped.

By this time I had met a beautiful American girl in the record shop. (I apologise for referring to all my girlfriends as beautiful, but in my experience anyone you share your body's secrets with becomes beautiful.) She was returning to Kansas City the next day so I only saw her the one time, for about ten minutes. I can't say I was especially enamoured, but she was insistent we keep in touch. A correspondence began, spanning more than a year. She wrote me ten-page letters doused in perfume and sent me seductive photos of herself. Except she was a devout Christian (no sex before marriage) and engaged to a farm boy who worshipped Ted Nugent. As I've said, I liked love and desire best when they took place in my imagination. Then I was never anything less than my greatest hits. The moment you carry your love and desire out into the physical world all your shortcomings begin to be pointed out. I enjoyed loneliness, yearning, sadness. They were probably my favourite states of mind – the equivalent of standing alone on an empty beach at sunrise when the tide is right out. It's only when I'm sad that I feel truly wise. Sadness, essentially, is the ghost of happiness. Happiness is always present in sadness, an elusive scent just outside the frame. I liked it when my feeling had to range wistfully over distances. Lori, my American girl, poeticised the future in my thoughts. She gave to my longings foreground detail and a depth of background, and she also allowed me to enjoy all the freedoms of my cherished solitude.

I quit my job and, like David, was claiming unemployment benefit at the local dole office. I wore makeup to sign on and always had to withstand a blizzard of hostility in that grim building. Most of our time now was dedicated to our musical aspirations.

David had a brief affair with a married woman. I was curious and a bit jealous. He said the chief thing he learned was that sex was less secret to older women. When it was over he possessed an air of standing higher on a ladder, of owning property out of bounds to me. He made me feel inexperienced by comparison. His first serious girlfriend was a girl called Tilly. She was a marvel, witty, eloquent, clever and beautiful. But David confided in me that he didn't much enjoy sex. I remember him once expressing a theory that our sexual and creative energies run through the same channels and have the same source. "In other words, the more sex we have the less creative we are," he said.

I also remember well one conversation I had with Tilly. "You're like a measure to David," she said. "I think half of him idolises you and wants your approval, but another half wants to beat you at your own game. And I think you're a bit the same with him. You both demand undivided attention. You both have the ability to make people feel singled out and vivid to themselves. I'd hate to see you two ever compete for the same prize."

"Just as well then I'm not in love with you," I said.

"Neither of you feel it does you credit to have a girlfriend. It's not how you like to see yourselves. You want to be seen as solitary, a law unto yourselves. David's almost too independent. His reliance on others is as indirect as he can make it. Even the way in which he shares a moment of pleasure is screened. He reminds me of my plant, trailing everywhere, but in a pot. He's also so acutely honest with the world that I wonder it hasn't already swallowed him whole. All the doubts he casts over himself - if anything were ever to make me angry with him it would be them. It's almost as if he's always asking me to become disillusioned with him."

These turned out to be prophetic words.

At this time a French girl I saw a few times told me I made love like a butterfly. It was said with affection, but it wasn't a compliment. Probably Tilly was right and I had always sought to feel superior to my sexual experiences. Or perhaps it was simply that I had an incapacitating fear of losing control. Something me and David had in common. In fact, he was worse than me. Always protecting his dignity. It was impossible to imagine David running or even playing. Of doing almost anything animals do. Really though, I think both David and I disliked owning to anything that made us inseparable from everyone else. We liked to see ourselves as outcasts, otherworldly. Bowie in *The Man Who Fell to Earth* was perhaps our ideal. And his character's initiation into sex was the beginning of his downfall in the film. Thus, we belittled and mocked sex as any kind of meaningful experience. Sex is the great equaliser in life. Whether you're rich or poor, smart or stupid, beautiful or ugly, the pleasure pitch of erogenous zones, the quality of orgasm is not affected. Sex gives everyone equal opportunity. Snubbing it was a form of snobbery on our part. There's a lot of facetiousness aimed at sex in David's lyrics on the first two albums. Another reason those two records were so unrelatable to our generation.

By this time we had put an ad in *Melody Maker* for a guitarist and that's how Billy came to join the band. He was an exemplary human being – generous and kind and, most importantly where David was concerned, uncomplaining. He also bore a remarkable resemblance with his dark corkscrew hair to Sylvain Sylvain of the New York Dolls – them again! - which pleased David. He was older than us and a much more accomplished musician. He provided us with an incentive to catch up. He was never comfortable wearing makeup, which came so naturally to us. He drew the line at lip gloss but was finally convinced to wear a little kohl under his eyes. By now, we had written about ten of our own songs. Usually David would come up with a few broken threads of melody and together we would sew them together into some kind of finished article.

We were all working class boys. We all hated Thatcher, we all hated racism, we all hated social inequality and chest-thumping nationalism. Our appearance was a political statement of sorts. We were obviously anti-establishment. In other words, we had all the credentials to be darlings of the left-wing music press. However, we never sought acceptance from our contemporaries; if anything, we wilfully shunned it. David wrote a song in French. Another song about fascism with oblique references to Liliana Cavani's film *The Nightporter*. We were happy to be alone in our own sequestered world. To be honest, most of what we did in those days was a pose. Our early music had little soul.

Our first gig as a five-piece was in a social club in Lewisham. There were six people in the audience. We afterwards found out they were all friends of Billy. The next couple of gigs we played - Goldsmith College and the Bridge House in Canning Town - weren't any more auspicious. But then outside the rehearsal studio one day a man introduced himself to us as a talent scout. He complimented us on our look. In fact, he seemed besotted with our appearance. He told us we had all the makings of stars even though, to our knowledge, he hadn't heard a note of our music. He asked us if we needed a manager. And that's how we joined forces with his partner, Reg Shaw. Reg had a perm and the physique and attendant vanity of the ageing sportsman. He was as steely and efficient as a getaway car. He had managed a few artists in the sixties, one or two of whom we had heard of. He drove a white Rolls Royce and favoured gold jewellery. He took us out to dinner at an expensive restaurant in Kensington. Told us we had to build up our confidence as performers and urged us to perform as many gigs as possible in the next year. "I've found in life it's more educational to make your mistakes in public." A terrible piece of advice. We soon realised he was completely out of touch with the British music scene, but we were flattered by the belief he had in us and his ability to create the illusion that he could see into the future. I was probably better at reading people's eyes than David, but not even I saw how much unscrupulous greed there was in Reg's soul. However, he played a big part in helping us to take ourselves much more seriously as artists. It was a moment of pride when I was able to tell my parents we had a manager who drove about in a Rolls Royce.

Reg was a master at commanding vaudeville insincerity, so important in the music industry. His voice was an advertisement of his virility and the steadiness of his hand. It was a voice primed for interruption. He genuinely enjoyed hanging out with us. Often took us out to dinner and revelled in the attention we attracted. His dealings with the bow-tied waiters drew attention to his emotional conceits: he liked to project himself as a man used to getting his own way. On the street, people would stop and stare at us, and he would tell everyone we would be famous in a year. Adopting his haughty air of entitlement - he was vain of his social prestige, of his ability to pull strings, open doors, ingratiate himself onto guest lists, elicit discounts in restaurants and shops - Reg always strode into officious buildings as if he was there to collect rent. I can see him now, raising his voice and waving a fork with a strawberry impaled on it at me.

We were naïve and signed binding contracts without knowing what we were renouncing. It never occurred to us to have a lawyer look over them. We also signed a publishing contract and

Reg convinced us it would legally be easier if all the songwriting was accredited to only one person. David wrote the lyrics and usually came up with the basis of a melody line so, on paper, he became the sole author of our music. However, many of our songs were initially arranged by me and Pete. I'd also argue that a good deal of the energy and creativity of our music was provided by me and Pete. I had begun to develop a melodious style of playing bass. In many of our songs, further down the line, the melody line I provided on the bass was just as distinctive as David's vocal melody line. But thus it was that David reaped all the royalties from our music throughout our career as a band. Had session musicians been used they would have earned more from our four albums than Pete, Alan, Billy and I did. People assume I made lots of money from my time in Orfée. Nothing could be further from the truth. David granted me half the royalties of the song 'Ghost Dance' on our final album though my contribution to that song was no more significant than my contribution to countless other songs. This gesture, I suspect, was prompted by the guilt for what he was doing behind my back at this time.

I've given a lot of thought to the question of royalties over the years. Who does a song belong to? If five friends go out and have a great time together should only one of them get all the credit for the memory made? Every song of ours was composed in a slightly different way. It's true there were a few where David's input far exceeded anyone else's, mostly the ballads. I feel a lot of love for the lyrics David writes now for his solo projects. But in the beginning his lyrics were often inane jargon he hid behind. *Statistics follow her footsteps/ a new crisis stands in line/ she is pale in the mirror/ my fingerprints on the crime.* That kind of thing. And for that he received 100% of every royalty that song made.

Soon Reg booked us into a studio in Denmark Street. He wanted three songs to play to people. We recorded 'The Laughter Inside', 'Your Voice' and 'Providence'. I remember the engineer praised Pete and me for how tight we were as a unit. It was perhaps the first meaningful compliment I had received for my musicianship. Its uplifting fallout didn't last long. Reg hawked the tape around London's record companies. No one was interested. One, I think it was CBS, advised the band to find a new bass player or at least teach the existing bass player how to put his fingers on the frets. This made everyone laugh. But it took me weeks to get over the hurt it caused me. Reg advanced us £10,000 and Pete bought a decent drum kit and I was able to buy a Wal fretless bass. We then began playing a lot of gigs in and around London. Usually supporting punk bands. We opened for Generation X, Tom Robinson, X-Ray Spex, the Vibrators, the Damned. (We went on to become more successful than any of the bands we supported, with the exception of Talking Heads.) We didn't go down well with the fans of any of these bands. Everyone on a stage was spat at in those days, but the nature of the spit we received was more belligerent and menacing. There was no youthful joie du vivre in it. And they refused to pogo, a sure sign we didn't meet with their approval. Every time I opened my mouth to sing a backing vocal I'd receive a blast of beery slobber and phlegm that I could taste in my mouth. One night, we had bottles thrown at us and David got so angry he smashed his guitar on stage at the end of the set. We'd return to the dressing room covered in beer and mucus. We were still very shy boys. It took every last ounce of our courage to step out onto a stage under lights. The makeup was our armour. We hid behind it. But it angered punks no less than it angered our fellow claimants in the dole queue. In the early days it was as difficult earning any open affection or praise from an audience as it had always been for me to earn these affirmations from my parents.

Punk though did have its influence on David. His vocal style became more drawlingly aggressive – most famously represented by his repeated full-throated scream on the title track of our second album *Climbing Trees*. His voice was still striving after a pitch that did not naturally belong to him. I liked this quality for a while. More than once David asked me to take away some of the attention on him on stage. He was struggling with being in the limelight. But I was having my own problems with stagefright. In the dressing room before every concert there was a moment when primeval panic threatened to sweep away all my footholds. The walk from the dressing room to the stage was always the loneliest walk of my life. It wasn't until the middle of the first song that I began to relax. David's inclination was to camp it up, emulate Bowie and Ronson's onstage erotica, throwing a limp-wristed hand over my shoulder and generally seeking physical contact with me whenever he felt nakedly exposed on stage. I never took to the camp charade. It was the bloody New York Dolls all over again. In an effort to conquer my nerves I created a persona of studied aloofness. I hid myself inside a shell. Inspired by *Blade Runner* I pretended I was an android. I faked the absence of a nervous system. I would smirk at David whenever he sidled up to me on stage as if it were a programmed response in my electronic circuitry.

At this time Lori, my American pen pal, told me she was getting married. I decided, without telling her, that I would go to Kansas City before the wedding date. I went to the American embassy to get a visa. I sold lots of my albums, most of them stolen, to a second-hand record shop in Soho for funds. David was quietly furious. He wasn't someone who ever got openly angry. His anger usually took the more measured form of facetious asides or a deflated blowing noise like air escaping from a badly tied balloon. Whenever he listened at length one of his manicured arched eyebrows lifted and gave to his entire face an expression of bemused intolerance. But my mind was made up. It always pained me when I disappointed him. But I needed to know how much reality there was in my feelings for Lori. And I wanted the moment of seeing the shock on her face. My imagination wasn't willing to venture beyond that moment. I gave no thought to possible repercussions. I promised I would be back in ten days. We had to cancel five gigs.

I got a flight to Chicago and then another flight to St Louis and then a Greyhound bus to Kansas City. I had never felt so alone, so cut adrift from habit. I found I enjoyed it, as if I had an entire stretch of ocean to myself. It felt strange being apart from David. I missed not being able to immediately share my thoughts and impressions with him. And without him and his moral support more courage was required of me to wear makeup. Especially because of the narrow-minded reactionary reputation of the American Midwest. Thus I toned down my appearance to some extent; I wasn't wearing lipstick, blusher or the red powder around my eyes I favoured when on stage; I was though wearing ivory foundation and eye-liner and my hair was dyed jet-black and kingfisher-blue. I arrived in the Country Club Plaza in the late afternoon of a scorching July day after an interminable bus journey during which a man at the back had announced he had a gun. No one took much notice of him. Lori worked in the clothes department of an elegant department store called Swanson's. Whenever I asked anyone directions they simply stared back at me in disbelief. One woman, incredulous, asked me if I was a boy or a girl, anticipating the moment, a lifetime of technological upheaval distant, when I would be asked the same question about Bysshe.

I was terrified when I entered the large store, but I also felt proud of myself. As if I was about to plant my flag on some pre-viously unexplored high peak. When Lori saw me, her blanched disbelief made me feel I had returned from the dead. I watched her body lurch back in bloodthumping bewilderment. I thought she might faint. So did one of her work colleagues who came over to intervene. She kept repeating her disbelief. Her wedding was in two weeks. The intensity of the moment was too much for both of us. We exchanged a hopscotch of inane remarks. I was so nervous I had only a child's vocabulary at my disposal, rudi-mentary verbs and adjectives, as if the primitive nature of my emotion had yet to evolve a sophisticated language. We finally arranged to meet for lunch the following day. I was, by turns, both elated and despondent after we parted. I still wasn't sure how much reality there was in my feelings for her as a person.

That night I left my hotel and went for a walk. I wandered into a leafy residential area, past a succession of expensive withdrawn houses where on every lawn a sprinkler sprayed a rotating glittering arc of water. There was no one else about. Until a car drove slowly past and then stopped just ahead. I could see three or four young males inside. They all had long hair. When I walked alongside they called me a faggot and threw an empty beer bottle at me. The car pulled off with more abuse and then stopped a hundred yards further ahead. My male pride was now being put to the test. I was stubbornly reluctant to display any show of open cowardice. So I walked on. Determined not to show any fear. Even though my legs were sagging with apprehension and my heart was thumping wildly. I was still walking towards them when I noticed a board advertising a nursing home at the edge of a lawn.

The woman at the desk gaped at me, as if I were an alien, just landed on planet earth. There wasn't a loose hair on her head; every strand was welded into a radioactive sculpture. There was more makeup on her face than I used in a month. Was her appearance really any less outlandish than mine? I gave up on her. I caught the eye of a curious black janitor. I recalled his face when, years later, I took up sculpture. His face was an eloquent and moving map of a hard life. I would have loved to have sculpted it. He called a taxi for me and sat with me outside on the doorstep while I waited for it to arrive. We talked about music. He kept looking at me, shaking his head and smiling.

I had lunch with Lori the next day in the Country Club Plaza, an elegant self-contained district of Spanish architecture with fountains everywhere. She kept telling me what we were doing was a sin. When she finished work we went to a bar and she drank rather a lot of red wine, forgot her guilt, forgot to keep bringing her fiancé into the conversation and we kissed before saying goodbye. We kissed again in a park the following evening and then had dinner together. Half way through the meal the Ted Nugent fiancé appeared. He grabbed Lori by the hair and shouted abuse at her. Then he changed his mind and turned his attention to me. He gripped me by the throat and began throttling me. Crockery and glasses were smashed in the ensuing scuffle. He eventually dragged Lori away. The entire restaurant was pulsating with heightened attention, all focused on me. I felt like I did onstage and resorted to my lopsided android smirk. In the aftermath I discovered my wallet was missing. I had no money to pay for our meal. The restaurant staff were sympathetic. I didn't have to wash any dishes. Lori restored my wallet to me the next day – Ted Nugent had stolen it for some reason. She told me he himself didn't know why. There was now no longer any question of spending time together of an evening.

Without doubt, Lori took me to emotional heights I had never reached before. I felt there was a shine on my body. And I was brimming with goodwill towards everyone I met. It was like spare change I was distributing to the less fortunate. But there were black holes in this new universe of exalted wellbeing I had entered. You might say I was bi-polar at this time. To climb higher is to risk falling from a greater height. And some of these falls, occurring when I was alone in my hotel room, knocked the stuffing out of me. The truth, which I was reluctant to admit because it seemed unworthy, was that I had no wish to get married, and this was the only option she appeared willing to grant me.

In the ensuing months, after I returned to London, I clocked up a two-thousand-pound phone bill, which I didn't pay until years later. Lori had cancelled her wedding. One minute, she was coming to London; the next, she didn't have it in her to take such a giant step. I thought I was going to have a nervous breakdown. Moments of euphoria were followed by crippling panic attacks. David was wise and immensely helpful. He helped me see I had no home for the emotions she made me feel. And that it was the drama I loved. I was in no way mature enough to sustain any kind of long term relationship. It's still something I haven't managed. To my confusion was now added guilt. I wasn't entirely sure my motives for disrupting a wedding were honourable.

I don't remember any of the gigs we played during this period, though there were a lot of them and often outside London, in cities and towns we had never visited before. Long drives up and down motorways in the back of a blue camper van. The rushing past of blurred and painted motorway lights at night might be the perfect image to represent what life on the road is like for a rock band. Mostly, time consists of inbetween transit moments. The van belonged to Mick who was our sound engineer, roadie, caterer, secretary and general dogsbody. We presumed Reg paid him a wage but never asked.

Then I learned from her sister that Lori had had a breakdown. That a doctor had told her to cut all ties with me. That I was making her ill. I was both relieved and devastated.

My depressed state over the demise of my relationship with Lori was provided with an antidote by the news that Reg had secured us a record deal, with a little-known German label whose other artists were all disco oriented. Meetings with lawyers, publicists, photographers, executives all followed. Our dream was finally being authorised.

David and I moved out of the flat in Greenwich, to escape the exorbitant phone bill as much as anything. We moved into a flat in the Fulham Road. We recorded the first album quickly. There were no arguments, but neither was there much inspiration. Having played them every night for months on end we had grown bored with all our songs by now. 30,000 posters were distributed before the album's release. More than once we saw one of these posters in some prestigious place – Chelsea, Soho, Notting Hill. The record company spent a lot of money promoting us. But the album was greeted with scorn and indifference in the music press. Mostly we were written off as dated glam rock. Julie Burchill slated it in the *NME*, referring to it as beautiful and damned melodrama. We began to headline gigs in London - The Marquee, The Greyhound in Fulham Road, Dingwalls in Camden Town, but few people came to see us. However, we were becoming more accomplished as musicians on stage. We wrote some new songs and for the first time the energy of our music began to run like lightning up and down my spinal cord until I was light-headed with the spell and elation of it. I was still petrified before walking on stage. But by the end of the set I was usually in a state of out-of-body euphoria and never wanted to leave the stage.

We were all in agreement in our loathing of our first album. We hadn't cleansed ourselves of our influences. At the time we took some consolation from how much misguided rubbish David Bowie produced before he achieved any artistic integrity. His early records and his mime performance 'The Mask' were colossally more humiliating than anything on our first record. Our second album, which we recorded six months later, was a bit better though David's lyrics became even more oblique and pretentious. Neither of them sold at all. And I think we might have been forced to split up at that point had it not been for Japan.

I can't remember now the moment we were told our debut album, released months later outside the UK, had sold 50,000 copies in Japan in the first week. Unknown to us, Reg had made sure photos of us were widely distributed to all the Japanese music magazines. As a result we had 30,000 members in our Japanese fan club weeks before the album was even released. Japan was weird in those days. The only contact Japanese kids had with western music was through photographs of artists in glossy colour magazines. Pop music wasn't played on the radio. Therefore they chose what bands to like almost exclusively on their image. You could say Japan was way ahead of its time in that regard. Nowadays, for the achievement of fame, image is often immensely more important than talent. But boy did Japanese girls love our image! Japanese magazines immediately sent over photographers to London and we did countless sessions for them. Soon we were getting lots of mail from Japan. All of it from girls and often wanting our babies. We learnt how much sex appeal we each possessed as individuals as a result of these letters. And probably there was some withheld jealousy. David was easily the most sought after. I was second followed by Pete and then Alan. Poor Billy barely got a look in. We ribbed him about it, but it must have hurt. It was like a survey had informed him he held no sexual attraction for the female sex. Reg quickly set up a tour of Japan.

We were greeted at Tokyo airport by a TV news film crew and hundreds of hysterical girls who screamed a high-pitch wall of sound while we were briefly interviewed, and then grabbed and tore at us as bodyguards escorted us to a white limousine. Of course we had seen film of this kind of thing happening to others, most notably the Beatles. But it both bewildered and embarrassed me that it was happening to us. We had done absolutely nothing to warrant it. We hadn't even written one decent song yet. Many of the girls followed us in taxis to our hotel. There were more girls waiting for us there and we had to be smuggled in via a service lift from the underground carpark. It was all dizzily surreal, like we had suddenly entered some alternate universe.

I shared a hotel room with David and we could see snow-capped Mount Fuji from our window, so high up were we.

The first few days were taken up with media activities: TV shows, tea ceremonies, photo sessions in temples and exotic locations, press conferences. Everything conspired to aggrandise us. In our own eyes though we struggled to believe we were worthy of all this attention as if we had been mistaken for someone else and before long the error would be registered. I even felt uncomfortable signing autographs. As if I were perpetrating a con trick. And everywhere we went we were followed by young girls in taxis. A lot of them didn't look old enough to have left school. We soon had to resort to deploying decoy taxis and crouching down below the windows.

In the hotel room we would hear giggling and whispering outside our door and receive intermittent calls from girls. One time I opened the door to two girls dressed only in leather jackets and panties. They both clawed at me and shrieked. I quickly shut the door on them. They haunted me for the rest of the night though, the glimpse I caught of their bared breasts and black laced panties, the possibilities they offered, the possibilities I declined. Another night Billy's curiosity got the better of him and he wandered out of his room in the middle of night. He said there were dozens of girls asleep on the stairs.

I ought to say something about groupies. Not once to my knowledge did any of us take immediate advantage of the girls offering themselves to us. With the exception, once or twice, of Billy. This caused David to take against him. David was our moral arbiter and something of a puritan at heart. Overall though, I reckon we might stake a claim to have been the most chaste band in the history of rock and roll. It's odd how girls will shed all their usual scruples and defence mechanisms, relinquish every demand to make you do any work for the gift of their sexuality just because you have a slice of fame. Then they tell the whole world afterwards as if they will rise in everyone's opinion. I always assume they are girls who can't have much self-esteem. However, it wasn't any kind of ethical consideration that compelled me always to walk away. I think I was intimidated as much as anything.

Sex, when it's offered on a platter, is one of the most difficult things in the world for a man to refuse. Almost every time I have refused it I've been persecuted by regret afterwards. It's a refusal that gives power to all kinds of doubts about your manhood. It often feels as though you have said no to life itself. I remember once, in a nightclub, I was talking to Pete when I felt a hand on the back of my thigh. Out of the corner of my eye I saw a mane of blonde hair, but I carried on talking to Pete as though someone caressing the inside of my thigh in a nightclub was an everyday occurrence. After a bit the hand moved away, and I never did discover who it belonged to. It began to bother me more and more though. When I got home I was furious with myself. I almost got a cab back to the nightclub in the hope of replaying the moment of temptation. Of course that's never possible. Women, quite rightly, have a scorn for men who act only with hindsight.

We played the Budokan later that week. It holds 15,000 people and we sold out two nights there; earlier in the month we had attracted less than 100 people to the Marquee in London. I couldn't see a single male in the audience. Just a screaming sea of young girls, jumping up and down and throwing soft toys, flowers, jewellery, coloured streamers and chocolates at us. I remember several times on stage we all exchanged bewildered looks. But of course we revelled in this pantomime of surging affection too. And once again I experienced the incomparable rush of exhilaration that comes with giving a good account of yourself on stage. The rapturous applause at the end of the set like a shot of unadulterated love pumped directly into a vein.

We were full of love for each other and for the world when we returned to the dressing room.

I remember how sobering it was arriving back in a rainy London where there were no TV crews waiting for us, no screaming girls, no limousines. I felt I would be happy living in Japan for the rest of my life.

It began to occur to us that, though we were selling out 15,000 seat venues, had notched up two top five albums in Japan, we were still sharing hotel rooms, travelling economy class and earning only fifty quid a week. It was the first inkling we had that Reg was pocketing most of the money we were earning. Thanks to Reg's extravagant lifestyle we were constantly in debt as a band. It bothers me now how expertly he performed the charade of projecting himself our friend and ally while simultaneously stealing as much of our money as he could get away with. (I suspect he also chalked up the occasional sexual conquest on the back of his association with us.) His split behaviour - I think he did genuinely enjoy our company - makes me think of that Scott Fitzgerald quote: "The test of a first-rate intelligence is to hold two opposing ideas in mind at the same time and still retain the ability to function." Reg was able to both admire us and think us gullible fools. I guess, by Scott Fitzgerald's standard, he had a first-rate intelligence.

6

Bysshe was in Stigma City, looking for Tobias Hives' detective agency. She was now idling in what appeared a scorched gangland neighbourhood. Script above her head declared '*I'm on Welfare*'. She swivelled around on her heels. Two eagle-eyed young men were standing in a shop doorway close by. The threat of violence gusted into the moment. Bysshe should have felt all the grounding weight leave her legs.

"Ninju thinks that Welfare must have upped its dividends to pay for such an elegant dress," said Ninju Pichot.

"Bysshe shoplifted it," said Bysshe, as if speaking in the third person was street etiquette here. I put her into a catwalk attitude: she looked askance at Ninju over a raised shoulder. He was standing with one heel raised and pressed to the graffitied wall behind him. Bysshe began to stomp with her usual manic panache down the menacing street. She looked like she was hunting someone down to do them harm.

"Ninju thinks he wouldn't go down there if he were you."

"Why?"

"Ninju knows dangerous people to be lurking in this hood."

"Bysshe likes dangerous people," lied Bysshe.

"Want some drugs?" shouted Ninju.

"Wouldn't know what to do with them."

"Ninju will give them to you anyway. You wear them."

Bysshe received a folder named MDMA, Ketamine, Crack, Smack, Coke and Pills.

When she turned a corner into another dystopian street full

of boarded-up houses and burnt-out vehicles I heard a faint meow. I noticed an avatar further up the dimly-lit road. It was scampering with bewitching agility along the pavement on its hands and knees. It came into clearer view and darted past Bysshe towards a firebombed warehouse. It was a she, naked save for a skimpy wink of red underwear. Her body appeared to be covered in dirt. She also had a tail which swung about like a fishing line. The grace and speed with which she moved about on her hands and knees mesmerised me. I heard another meow in my speakers and caught a glimpse of her name, Fuschia Nyo. Bysshe was smitten and set about following her. The sky darkened and there was a sudden downpour of rain. I had the feeling Fuschia had made it rain. I had the feeling Fuschia was a kind of necromancer and there might be things I could learn from her.

Bysshe could not keep pace with Fuschia's wildcat speed and agility and I quickly lost sight of her. Bysshe was now standing by an abandoned heavily stained mattress. Next to it was a pink poseball – *masturbate-(f)*. I clicked on it and Bysshe began performing catatonic gyrations with her head thrown back. She didn't look like she was masturbating; she looked like she had just gripped an exposed power line with both hands.

Bysshe marched up another street of broken windows and strewn rubbish. There seemed to be lots of lag tonight. An impeding force-field which created walls where visually there were no walls. She passed a telephone kiosk, a basketball court and an empty bar. Still no sign of Tobias Hives' detective agency. A low desolate sucking noise was coming out of my speakers. It sounded like moving air trapped in a tunnel. Bysshe walked towards a door next to a filling station. The next thing I knew she had passed through a wall and was standing in a men's lavatory. It was not the kind of lavatory you'd want to find yourself in in real life. There were poseballs scattered around the urinals – *piss whore, dominant, receive*. All my self-consciousness returned. I was no longer Bysshe; I was Nick, sitting alone at home with a urinal on my computer screen offering glory holes, male to male anal sex and piss whores. It didn't look good. This was not how I liked to think of myself. In fact, I could think of few things I had done in my life that, viewed from a kind of spectator grand-stand, were more demeaning to my sense of self. And I couldn't rid myself of the suspicion that someone somewhere might be covertly spying on my activities. It crossed my mind that they might call the police.

Then I saw that Fuschia had joined Bysshe in the nightmare lavatory. Her presence made me jump, as if a small animal had furtively scurried across the room in which I sat. This was the closest up I had yet seen her. She was standing with her back to Bysshe but looking over her shoulder at her. Her tail was whip-ping back and forth. Her black hair reached almost down to her waist. She looked as though she hadn't enjoyed a communion with water in weeks.

"Hello. My virgin moon bride."

"Hi," said Bysshe. I was pleased Bysshe seemed relaxed and playful because this wasn't how I felt. I was a bit weirded out.

The two girls spent an electric few moments studying each other. My imagination strained to develop an image of the person at the keyboard of the other computer. The intimacy was somehow so thick that I felt as though Fuschia's owner was trailing fingertips down the curve of my spine. Fuschia did her lithe cat crawl across the stained tiles and leapt up onto one of the damaged sinks. There was the sound of dripping water and the low desolate wind noise.

"You make me feel very shy," said Bysshe.

"Meow," purred Fuschia. There was a kind of heightened vitality about Fuschia Nyo as if everything she touched gave her a mild electrical shock.

"I like this place."

"I prefer sea views," said Bysshe.

"Shall I make you happy?"

"Half way through a cigarette I am already craving a new one," said Bysshe. "Contentment is wasted on me. It scares me, or I find I'm not quite ready for it and want to return to the moment prior to its arrival."

"Take off your wedding dress, Bysshe."

Bysshe did as she was told. She was now wearing the armoury of Victorian undergarments which had come with the wedding dress.

"I want to see you naked."

"I don't have nice skin." I was genuinely insecure about Bysshe's nudity. Most of the female avatars I had seen naked possessed photographically realistic flesh which I imagined you had to buy and was expensive. Bysshe's breasts had greyish nipples, her pudendum had no detail.

A message appeared: Fuschia Nyo has given you a body part named 'slut skin-complete.'

"For next time," said Fuschia. "Kneel down in front of me."

I right-clicked on the pink poseball *kneel* and Bysshe was down on her knees with her head between Fuschia's legs. The two avatars swayed in synchronised movement. Fuschia's head rolled back in ecstatic abandon. It crossed my mind that Fuschia might be a man in real life; that here we were, two men engaged in a simulacrum of a lesbian ritual.

"I've just lost my SL virginity," said Bysshe.

"I have to go. My master is about to summon me."

"Master?"

"I'm a kajira."

"You speak in riddles."

"Gorean slave."

"Gorean? What's that?"

"Google it hun."

And Fuschia vanished.

I took Bysshe off to Luna, a place I liked where tram tracks ended and the sea was nearby. The experience with Fuschia had made me feel a bit grubby, as if I had touched a stranger's dirty washing. I was googling 'kajira' when a boy called Hans Loon in a floral shirt arrived and was studying Bysshe with benevolent bewilderment.

"Sorry," he said.

"Hast any philosophy in thee, Shepherd?" asked Bysshe.

"Ich lade auf dir."

"It's no good you talking to me in German."

"DEUTSCH."

"I know that."

"Ich ner deutsch."

"You really must stop talking to me in German, Mr Loon."

"OK. Have fan."

"You have fan too. You're a sweet boy," called out Bysshe as he wandered away. "I can tell."

I felt a warm glow of liking for Hans Loon that had no rational armature. It was baffling how you could get a sense of someone here with barely any assistance from your five senses. It had nothing to do with the visual effect of the avatar behind which the person hid. Rather, it was as if there were an unseen unheard transmission of coded signals passing back forth in the ether, particles of electrochemical energy which somehow conveyed as cargo the aura of the people hiding behind their cyberspace envoys. I've always believed first impressions are paramount in life. That we have access to much we need to know about a person in the blink of an eye. That everything subsequently publicised is a confirmation of knowledge already fermenting in the distillery of the unconscious. Heightened curiosity discloses and absorbs a wealth of coded information. Which is why I believe more or less everything fateful begins in feeling, not in fact.

I had sent an instant message to Tobias Hives, the private investigator, asking for an appointment and was waiting for his reply. Kirsty had told me he had caught her husband in a dungeon, strapped to some kind of rack with a black hood over his head. Tobias had teleported Kirsty to the scene just as her husband was having the handle of a whip rammed up his rectum. She was now, she told me in a triumphant pageant of moral indignation, filing for divorce.

I was excited and nervous about the appointment with

the private investigator. There was no denying the chemical reactions in my bloodstream were no less organic than those produced by real life anticipation.

Tobias Hives was sitting behind a polished wooden desk when Bysshe tumbled down into his office.

"Hehho," said Tobias.

"Hehho," returned Bysshe.

"Sorry, I meant to type hello. Please take a seat."

Bysshe sat down and asked if she could smoke.

"I'd rather you didn't. What can I do for you?"

I had elaborated the story I would pitch while driving my delivery van from one address to another in West Sussex.

"Basically, I've got this bet going with a friend," said Bysshe.

"Go on."

"Well, we both have avatars in Second Life and we're having a contest to see who can find the other one first."

"Sounds like fun."

"Yes. Except I've decided to cheat a bit and hire you to find her."

"Just shows initiative if you ask me."

"So I want you to find out her avatar's name."

"I see."

"Will that be possible?"

"Could be. I'll need some details of course."

"What kind of details?"

"Let's start with her email address."

A little sheepishly I had told Linda about my quest to find our daughter in this virtual world. She, reasonably, asked me why I didn't just send her an email. "If she's alive and well and has access to the internet she'll read her emails." I rebuffed by reminding her that Katie didn't respond to her emails. Linda said: "She doesn't want to talk or listen to me. I wrote to her telling her I had found you. Nothing. Send her an email with the subject "I'm your father". If she's ever online she'll definitely read that." The truth, however, was that I didn't want to make things so easy for myself; I was enjoying the challenge of seeking her out in this virtual world. It seemed appropriate that I should be made to work to establish contact with my unknown daughter. Sending her an email felt like cheating. I wanted her to know I was willing to go to adventurous lengths to find her. I was about to type Katie's email up on the screen when Tobias said:

"But before we go any further we should talk about fees."

"Okay."

"I charge $100 an hour plus expenses, to be paid always in advance."

"I see."

"So before we go any further I will have to ask you for $100."

"Not American dollars?"

"No. Lindens. You'll find the exchange rate is usually about 250 lindens to one US dollar. So let's say it takes me 48 hours to find out your friend's avatar's name that'll work out at about twenty dollars."

"Sounds reasonable."

"So you want me to go ahead?"

"Yes please. But I'll have to get some money."

"Do you know how to do that?"

"Not really."

"Okay, I'm sending you an LM (landmark) where there are cash machines. You go there, click on the machine and follow the instructions. You've got a cash or debit card?"

"A real one?"

"Yes."

"I do."

"You use that. In the meantime give me the email address and I'll get the ball rolling. When you've got the money bring up on my profile and click on PAY."

Not for the first time the protocols of this world were returning me to the untutored innocence of a child. I realised it was not uncommon for me here to act and feel as though I was yet to experience myself as an adult. I suspect this godly power a virtual world has to restore youth plays a major part in its appeal for many people.

"Thank you very much, Mr Hives."

"My pleasure."

Over the next couple of days Tobias Hives kept me informed about his progress. He had written Katie an email with a bogus Second Life address in which he was proud to announce that she had won a 2,000 linden dollar cash prize for being the sexiest female avatar some market research team had spotted during their virtual travels. She only had to reply to his email confirming her avatar's name to receive her prize. Tobias informed me that most people were outlandishly vain about their avatars. He proved to be right because it worked. Katie's avatar was named Alaya Twine. I immediately called Linda, not realising it was three thirty in the morning, and told her it would appear our daughter was alive and well.

Bysshe, wearing a crushed red velvet dress and a red head-scarf, returned to Tobias' office.

"I did a little extra surveillance work. For a further $5,000 I can let you have some info which will help you find her. Alaya is heavily into Gor and there are hundreds and hundreds of Gorean sims so you'd still have a problem finding her without this information."

"What is Gor?"

"Hard core roleplaying based on sci-fi books written years ago. Lots of master/slave sex relationships and lots of fighting. They use combat meters, scripted weapons and have strict dress codes. They take it very seriously."

"Ok."

"We have a deal?"

I paid Tobias Hives. I had now made him $20,000 richer. Thankfully that was only virtual money and added up to about seventy quid in the real world.

"You sure you want to hear this?"

Bysshe blinked. "Oh, yes please."

"Well, Alaya is presently the captive of someone called Nomedo Arumi who is what's known as "the first sword of Argentum". Argentum is a city in Gor. If you want to surprise her there my advice would be to read up about Gor before going there. They'll eject and ban you if you don't obey the rules."

I googled Gor. I can't say what I read made my understanding any clearer. Apparently, the man who wrote the Gor novels believed the industrial revolution stifled man's natural instinct to be more dominant and woman's natural instinct to be more submissive. There had been no industrial revolution in Gor. Women were often slaves known as kajira. If they weren't slaves, they were required by law to cover up all flesh including their faces. The only other alternative for a female was to join a tribe of wild huntresses who lived in the woods, shunned male company and were known as panthers.

I asked Arana what she knew about Gor. Surprising me with the vehemence of her reply, she told me she found the whole thing repulsive. She told me she had once been a kajira, a collared slave. She told me that Bysshe would only be allowed to visit Gor as a free woman in which case she would have to wear a veil but would still have to abide by the laws of the place. On the whole she sought to dissuade Bysshe from venturing there alone, as if it were mined with fatal consequences.

I typed Argentum into the map search. It was part of a large six-sim land mass. I decided to send Bysshe to the sim furthest away from Argentum itself so she would have a longish walk before she reached the city and, in that way, perhaps get the hang of the etiquette and how to roleplay. When she was standing on a little wooden landing stage on the bank of a wide river surrounded by hills I instant messaged Arana with the news that Bysshe was standing on Gorean territory for the first time.

"You really shouldn't do that until you know the rules," came back the reply. "What are you wearing?"

"My crushed red velvet dress with accessories," said Bysshe.

"You can't wear that! You must show some respect. I'll send

you a dress to wear. And you absolutely MUST wear a veil. Also wear gloves and smart shoes. I'll send you those as well. And whatever you do don't wear a combat meter. Wear an observer tag."

"Why?"

"You'll get attacked and have a collar put on you. There are lots of really nasty males in Gor. If you want to serve a master make sure you find one who's half way decent."

Bysshe changed into the dowdy brown dress and put on the veil Arana had sent her. She looked like a widowed Victorian bride, except there was no grief in the jaunty sing-song syncopation of her stride. I decided the veil didn't suit her so took it off. A sign informed her she was about to leave a safe zone and venture into a combat zone. I decided it was Bysshe's nature to be bold and adventurous, not timid and veiled. I clicked on an icon to receive a combat meter. As Bysshe marched with her usual careless manic abandon over the threshold I felt some fear and concern for her safety. I kept my eyes peeled. The hairs on my arms were alert to danger.

She followed a winding path with thick high tangled ferns on either side. My speakers emitted shrill insect and bird noises. Before long Bysshe reached a lake by which a wooden raft was moored. She stepped onto it and spied a solitary figure on the far bank. They spent a few tense moments studying each other. I wondered how quickly he could get across the lake to attack her. I then saw there were two other avatars swimming across the water towards him. I had never seen an avatar swim before. Bysshe certainly couldn't swim. She could though perform her ungainly walk beneath water, which is what I made her do now. I couldn't see what was happening on the far bank while she was stomping along on the bed of the lake, but I could hear a succession of pained male grunts. When Bysshe emerged from the water, two scantily clad females ran nimbly past her in pursuit of the bare chested, heavily tattooed male avatar. They were all firing arrows at each other some of which landed on the ground around Bysshe's feet. Typescript then began appearing on my screen -

Gorean Meter 2.6 shouts: Clovis Kingmaker has been defeated by Zula Woller and is dying.

Zula Woller stands over her prey and kicks him in the groin.

Gypsy Pollen sits astride the wounded prisoner and pushing his feet together takes her rope and ties it around his ankles several times in a secure knot.

Gorean Meter 2.6: Clovis Kingmaker has been bound into captivity.

Not much of this happened visually – or rather it happened in abrupt transitions without the intervening detail: one minute poor Clovis Kingmaker was lying crumpled on the ground with an eerie bubble around him proclaiming him unconscious, the next he was jerked to his feet with ropes binding his hands and ankles. One of the females had hold of him by a leash. All three figures had ignored Bysshe until now. It was apparent Bysshe was a foreigner here. Somehow she had slipped through customs, but her papers were far from in order. Neither could she master the language. She would have to rely on the kindness of strangers.

Zula Waller shouts: ((put a meter or observer tag on, Bysshe))

Gypsy Pollen: ((got a meter?))

"Why are you talking in brackets?" Bysshe asked.

Gypsy Pollen: ((OOC. You should be doing the same))

"What's OOC?"

Gypsy Pollen: ((Out of character hun))

Zula Waller: ((You need to read the rules))

"Actually, I have a meter," said Bysshe.

Gypsy Pollen: ((then wear it))

Zula Waller: ((you need to get rid of your tag too. No welfare in Gor. Lol))

Bysshe Artaud: Will you attack me?

Gypsy Pollen: ((maybe))

Bysshe watched as the two huntresses in their g-strings and

animal fur accessories dragged the captive male through the woods. They moved much more quickly and elegantly than Bysshe was able to. Like Fuschia, they had superior animations to the rank and file of Second Life citizens. I decided to obey the rules and wear the combat meter. This done I was asked if Bysshe was male or female. I was told the region was synchronized and it had "weaker female option enabled and stronger melee weapons". Bysshe didn't appear at all daunted by the bewildering obtuseness of this information.

As Bysshe marched heedlessly through the wilds of Gor, I realised I might now be about to talk to my daughter for the first time. I tried to form a picture of all the electrochemical activity in my brain. The neurotransmitters ferrying electrical signals across synapses to a succession of neurons, the synthesis of a firework burst of proteins. Visually I imagined it to resemble one of those speeded up films of a city at night. These pictures however seemed to cheapen my feeling so I aborted them. I did not like to think of Katie as some kind of hardwired genetic instruction. My feeling for her was, I liked to think, now the quest of my soul. It weighed twenty-one grams and was independent of molecular biology. I was both proud of this feeling and sceptical of it. As if it still needed the authorisation of an independent body to pass it as law.

Bysshe, alone again, hiked across a barren tract of land, crossing streams and climbing hills. There's a little radar map on the top right-hand side of the screen which shows any avatars in your vicinity. Suddenly there was a flurry of fidgeting green dots on the map. I felt an influx of nervous energy prickling my fingertips. I could see a group of figures standing on a high pass over a turbulent river and as Bysshe edged closer script began to roll down on my screen. (Bear with me because I'm including all the typos.)

Solstice Denja: Just now all i yearn for is to kneel by her grave....and my scalding tears to wetten the seeds i will plant by her side...till roses are nourished by my own pain...

Myst Zerbino: If you wish to go now Solstice, i will take you.

Solstice Denja: Take me now...and all who would come with me....

Myst was a hooded figure of indeterminate sex; Solstice was a handsome warrior with a poetic swagger about him. He was wearing a pleated black kilt and had a red ribbon tied around his forearm.

Solstice Denja: i must go to my sisters side...even in death... his eyes brimming with tears that have yet to water her grave... come then....

Myst Zerbino leads the way.

I was a bit miffed they had all ignored poor Bysshe. She herself though didn't seem offended and followed the group a few paces behind.

Phoenix Weyland studies the male in black. "You're a bounty hunter, you say?"

Marto Slade shrugs.

Phoenix Weyland: May I ask if you presently hunring anyone?

Phoenix Weyland: (hunting)

Marto Slade ignores the question, but instead looks over his shoulder at the suspicious female in the ugly brown gown who is following. He draws his dagger.

Marto Slade: Stop! Who are you?

Bysshe Artaud: Me?

Marto Slade has an urge to cut her just for her stupidity. "Why is your face uncovered?"

Bysshe Artaud: I was robbed in the hills yonder. They took my veil and all my money.

Marto Slade grabs the girl by the throat. "You lie."

Solstice Denja: Stop that! Cannot you see this is a sorrowful occasion?

Marto Slade: Pfft

Solstice Denja: Tonight there shall be peace among us all. Come my wild angel. I shall be glad of your company...

Bysshe Artaud: Thank you.

Myst Zerbino: Here she lays by this tree, sighs.

Phoenix Weyland turns his eyes to the sky in silent prayer.

I thought at this point I would add some purple prose of my own.

Bysshe Artaud stands by a pool overhung with bushes looking at the faint mound beneath the tree. As she imagines the dead girl who lays beneath that earth she becomes aware of the blood coursing through her own arteries.

Myst Zerbino: im sorry i couldnt do more, sighs.

Solstice Denja: i nod softly and gently kneel before the tree, my eyes searching up towards the heavens, knowing that my sister lies there in her own star, in her own moons crystal tear that dances the satined night alive....she has returned to become one with it…

Marto Slade: Your sister was murdered by who?

Solstice Denja: to become one with it and shine in eternity, in its shimmering gaze towards the world....softly i lay around her the seeds that i brought with me...blue roses as unique as she was...and i let the northern breeze scatter them…

Myst Zerbino places her hand on Solstice's shoulder. "She loved you dearly."

Marto Slade: I'm out of here.

Solstice Denja: i will seek him whose heart killed hers...in this life or the next....

Myst Zerbino: i wish for Solstice could have his sister back.

Solstice Denja: smiles* i have to go..its 4.00am and i am on long shifts....looks to Bysshe…Angel with those feline beautiful eyes that whisper to my own eyes the promise of an angels smile...do not forget me…

Bysshe Artaud blushes.

Marto Slade, Bysshe's persecutor, now stood by a bush with his arms limp at his side and his head flopped forward like a ventriloquist's doll. *Away* was written above his head.

Solstice evaporated in a shower of glitter, but not before he had accepted Bysshe's friendship request.

Despite all its madcap make-believe, I found I was drawn in and excited by this new world, in the same kind of way I had been when visiting France for the first time as a young boy. It's exciting to dramatise oneself in the custody of a new culture. Errors you make, shortcomings you display, are accepted and easily brushed off; they don't adhere to you the way they do on native turf. The exotic incantations of a new language can sound like magic formulas and make what might happen next unpredictable. Nothing can so easily be taken for granted. And Solstice's narrative held some interest for me. Would it be continued tomorrow? Would he set out to track down the man whose heart had killed his sister? I could think of many things, like going to work tomorrow, I'd less like to do than accompany Solstice on his quest. I had discovered people created stories in this world. And no one can argue that stories aren't powerful and compelling. I felt I was beginning to understand how this place might hold an attraction for my daughter. And that it might be my fault, transited from me to her in DNA.

Bysshe, once again alone, crossed a meadow where there were some strange animals and a stone circle. Arana had warned me that some of the animals in Gor could attack and kill you. I kept a wary eye on them. There was a menacing black fort perched high on a rocky crag. Bysshe arrived at a drawbridge and entered a large fortified city. Huge slabs of stone paved the dark streets which were lit by oil lamps. There was a howling of wind, rising and falling on a desolate note. The city was dissected by canals and the soft lapping of water could be heard behind the lament of the wind. The occasional rugged long-haired male figure armed with a sword and a bow strode about the streets, followed by one or two scurrying slave girls. Every time the male came to a halt, the girls knelt at his feet with upturned palms resting on their widely spread thighs. They were virtually naked save for fluttering strips of silk. Each wore a collar around her neck, some kind of metal garter on her right thigh and had a tattoo on her upper thigh. One slave girl was pulled along on a chain which made a tinkling noise in my speakers. The men were all dressed in swashbuckling medieval outfits.

My pulse was shooting up as I scanned the city streets and squares for Alaya Twine. I was reminded of the dizzying melee of my anticipation when I went to surprise Lori in Kansas City.

Soon I was eavesdropping on a conversation going on between three slave girls.

Consuela Akina: i was the queen escort when i started. i was and still am pretty good too when i need the lindens i was making 6000 a session and i have a client list thats a book :-)

Shanaa Zauber: Wow

Consuela Akina: but it was kink

Shanaa Zauber: online sex?

Consuela Akina: Yup girl

Tala Aslan: 6000 euro must be camera?

Consuela Akina: linden not euro. I wasn't that good…lol

Consuela Akina: but I'd get the guy to cumm in 10 minutes… lol

Shanaa Zauber: Men pay you to have virtual sex?

Consuela Akina: pay in advance of course

Tala Aslan: 15 minutes of voice is 4000L with the top voice escorts

Shanaa Zauber: You hear their voice too?

Consuela Akina: yeah i didnt get into the voice thing. after my first try i nearly threw up

Shanaa Zauber: I bet

Consuela Akina: but never cam…that shit ends up on the internet

Zoot Empire: ((Can you carry out your conversation in IMs? You're ruining the ambience with this OOC chatter.))

Tala Aslan: Yes, master. This girl humbly begs forgiveness.

Zoot Empire: ((Bysshe, you need to wear a veil and get rid of the welfare tag))

Bysshe Artaud: ((Sorry. On it now))

I removed the *'I'm on Welfare'* tag above Bysshe and restored the veil to her face.

In contrast with the elegant animations of all the other avatars I was by now so ashamed of Bysshe's graceless catatonic way of walking that I probably would have gone to great lengths to disassociate myself from her had this been real life. Her arms and legs scythed the air like scissors, putting me in mind of some over-zealous fascist official on a regimental parade ground. She also performed the humiliating pantomime of typing onto an imaginary keyboard when talking which none of her fellow companions in Gor did. I discovered they all had animation overrides, scripts which replaced and significantly sophisticated the standard movements of your avatar. I decided I would have to buy one before logging off. I didn't want Bysshe to give the impression to my daughter of being some kind of hapless coarse yokel.

Bysshe stomped past wooden market stalls with cloth canopies and then entered an inn. Sitting on a cushion in front of an open fire with a slave girl snuggled up in his lap was Nomedo Arumi, supposedly my daughter's lord and master. I felt my mouth go dry and gummy, as if I had been licking envelopes. He was a handsome devil – shoulder-length black hair, flickering green eyes, good bone structure. Bysshe ambled over to him.

"Tal Lady," he said. He wiped his mouth with a gloved hand.

"May I?" asked Bysshe. I wondered if he had meant to type 'Tall Lady' and felt momentarily insecure about Bysshe's height. Did I need to shrink her a bit? (I later learned 'tal' is Gorean for hello.)

"May you what?"

"Warm my hands at the fire," said Bysshe.

Tabitha Fabre slips out of her master's lap, scooting down his legs to the floor at his feet. Her red silks fluttering as they fall back into place at her ankles. She is jealous of master's interest in the beautiful lady. She looks up to her master, blue eyes glazed over with love, whispers something only she can hear.

Very rarely was an avatar to be seen doing what described. Pretty little Tabitha Fabre, for example, did jump up from Nomedo's lap and did fall down on her knees with her silk ribbons aflutter, but it would be visually inaccurate to say her eyes glazed over with love or that she was seen to whisper something only she could hear.

The two slave girls were now hogging the chat stream. Everything they were supposed to be doing was elaborately and dyslexically described. How one girl had to get the other girl a crate she could stand on to reach the top shelf where the best goblets were kept, how the goblets were reddish with a gold trim, how the chosen goblet was closely inspected for flaws, how the goblet was filled with vintage wine. It wasn't a compelling narrative. There was no story in it. I thought it a shame Solstice didn't enter the inn with his talent for drama. Nomedo, in comparison, had so far shown little charm or flair for invention. He just sat there, like some middle man between assignments. I decided it was time for Bysshe to speak up.

Bysshe Artaud: May I ask how many slaves you have, sir?

Nomedo Arumi: Only two at present, Lady.

Bysshe Artaud: May I be permitted to ask their names?

Nomedo Arumi: Why?

Even through the optic fibres I could sense Nomedo's brows furrowing with a hint of suspicion. I felt sure he was now looking at Bysshe's profile. Looking for clues as to my real life identity. An instant message then arrived. It was from Tala Aslan. The chirpy twice reiterated tone announcing incoming post startled me, making me realise how keyed-up I was. It said, Hi. Nothing else. It was quickly followed by another one -

IM: Tala Aslan: You're new, aren't you?

IM: Bysshe Artaud: Yes. Is it fun being a slave?

IM: Tala Aslan: Great fun. I love it.

IM: Bysshe Artaud: What's Nomedo like?

IM: Tala Aslan: He's kind of strict, but nice when you get to know him. You thinking of submitting to him?

IM: Bysshe Artaud: Maybe. Would I have to have sex with him?

IM: Tala Aslan: giggles

IM Tala Aslan: He's about to leave the tavern. Follow him and offer yourself. And be demur. He's very sweet, but he can be suspicious.

IM: Bysshe Artaud: Bit nervous about this slave business.

IM Tala Aslan: Stop being such a granny. *giggles

The idea occurred to me that Tala had been messaging Nomedo at the same time she was messaging me, and Nomedo had purposefully left the tavern as part of a plan to lure Bysshe into their plot. Paranoia, I was discovering, was a frequent companion in this virtual world. I was surprised by the kick of my nervousness as Bysshe took her leave of the inn. Nomedo was already some way off in the distance. He looked like he might be whistling to himself. He had left the city by a back gate in the walls and was strolling in a rural landscape of swelling and subsiding hills. Bysshe set off in his wake. Visually, the young girl following the solitary man along country paths, was compellingly fateful. It was a bit like a scene from a Thomas Hardy novel. *Tess of the D'Urbervilles* was an early favourite novel of mine. I loved its tragic depiction of romantic love. It also brought home to me how stuck in our ways, self-righteous and greedily insensitive we men can be. It remains the most artistically powerful feminist novel I've ever read.

Nomedo came to a halt at a building on the crest of a small hill. He was standing by the side of some kind of fowl coup.

"Have I interrupted you in a private moment?" asked Bysshe.

"I have some chores to attend to, Lady."

"You are feeding the chickens?"

"No. I am moving the coup, Lady. And they are vulo. ((No chickens in Gor)) Can I be of service to you?"

"Might I ask if you find me pleasing to the eye?" asked Bysshe shamelessly.

"How should I know while you remain hidden to me behind your veil, Lady?"

"Shall I take it off?"

"Only if you're willing to face the consequences."

"What would you think if I took it off?"

"I'd probably think you were coming onto me, Lady."

"If I took my dress off I'd be coming onto you."

Nomedo Arumi raises His eyebrows and a faint smile appears on His lips.

I thought about making a joke of his habit of capitalising all of his self-referring pronouns, but then remembered the slave girl's advice to maintain a demure attitude in his company.

"I would like to offer myself as a slave," said Bysshe.

"You wish to be my kajira?"

"If it so pleases you."

IM: Nomedo Arumi: How old are you?

IM: Bysshe Artaud: In real life?

IM: Nomedo Arumi: Yes.

IM: Bysshe Artaud: 23. (I still felt, in my solitary self, I was about twenty-three.)

IM: Nomedo Arumi: What sex are you?"

IM: Bysshe Artaud: ?

IM: Nomedo Arumi: We sometimes get males here pretending to be females. Are you female?

Bysshe Artaud: Yep. My period arrived yesterday to reaffirm the fact.

IM: Nomedo Arumi: Don't use chat when you're OOC. Use IM

IM: Bysshe Artaud: Sorry.

Nomedo Arumi: Very well, girl. I shall offer you a week's trial as my kajira.

IM: Nomedo Arumi: Do you know how to serve?

IM: Bysshe Artaud: No, but I'm a quick learner.

IM: Nomedo Arumi: You will ask my first girl to help you.

"I am most honoured."

"You must always refer to me now as Master."

"Yes, Master."

"You will be red silk. A pleasure slave."

"Yes, Master."

"Are you ready to submit yourself to me now?"

When he had asked Bysshe her sex an unpleasant shiver had gone through me, like when on a winter's night you roll onto a puddle of wet semen that has gone cold on the sheet. I also felt a bit sorry for the deceived Nomedo. Now, I realised I was genuinely uncomfortable about the prospect of performing cybersex with a male. The idea of being penetrated by a man, even if it took place through the medium of pixelated avatars, gave me the creeps. Bysshe was most happy as a lesbian – that much was very clear to me. She didn't want her pot of gold plundered by any man.

The real world sun had showed itself above the line of terraced rooftops visible from my window. I looked down at the time. It was six thirty in the morning. I had spent nearly ten consecutive hours with Bysshe. I had to be at the supermarket depot in less than an hour. I also hadn't been feeling well for a couple of days.

"I'm a bit nervous, master. Would it be possible for me to make a final decision tomorrow?"

"As you wish. I bid you good day."

7

Not long after returning from Japan we did a short tour of Italy. That is one of my favourite memories of the band. There was none of the mayhem or adulation of Japan, but as a band we had never been closer, more infatuated with each other. And, as musicians, our chemistry had reached a new height of bewitchment. In Japan all the euphoria seemed artificially induced. In Italy we felt the audiences, small as they were, were genuinely uplifted by our music. I thought back to the early days when David and I had sat with our guitars in his bedroom. Music then had been a foreign language. We only knew about thirty words. Barely sufficient to make ourselves understood. Now it was as if we had finally become fluent in this new language. And mastering a new language is one of life's great joys. It refreshes the way you experience yourself.

After every gig and a meal - restaurants in Italy are one of the best treats life has to offer - we always made a point of walking around every Italian city we played in. Usually we would remain outside until the sun came up. Thus we explored Palermo, Florence, Venice and Rome, always with the elation of a successful performance still buzzing in our blood. In Rome's empty streets I remember church bells turning over the dark air as a shovel turns over soil, naked resounding chimes that exalted the narratives of the gleaming ancient stones amongst which they echoed. (Later in life, my experience of Rome would be of a city which lifts you up but won't let you settle down – it can turn you into a bird without a nest.) In Venice I remember entering

Piazza San Marco at some point towards sunrise. We had it all to ourselves. It was swept clean and seemed to have great expectations of us. There was a kind of grandeur about the fact that we were the only people in the entire world who were standing on this historic stage. I felt as though I was being told a momentous secret, but was too drunk on life and tired to understand it. We didn't dare walk about in Naples after midnight as we were warned the Mafia might kidnap us!

When we returned from Italy David wrote three new songs, and when he played them to us we knew something transfiguring was about to happen. He had finally found a rich vein of creative inspiration in his soil. He had begun writing on the piano which, he said, helped him better understand chord structures and melody. I was electrified with jealous gratitude. I immediately began composing bass lines for them. His flurry of inspiration continued and soon we began recording our third album, *The Touch of Ghosts*. Finally, we had found our identity as a band. Alan's growing creative mastery of sequencers was a major factor here. He and David spent a lot of time together in the studio programming the synthesisers. We were much less guitar orientated now. And Pete and I could now claim to be one of the most accomplished and innovative rhythm section in pop. Pete had a melodic, spatially creative way of playing the drums. It was now that the prominence of the bass against the vocals became one of the trademark features of our music. Sometimes Pete and Alan thought the bass was too loud against the rest of the track. But David usually took my side in these disputes. The bass was often allowed to take a lead role. I had succeeded in giving the bass a much more melodic role and bringing it out of the background to the forefront. I had also learned the saxophone and clarinet and played both instruments on this album as well as arranging their parts. Thanks to my geisha girl shuffle back and forth across the stage and my lopsided android smirk, I had also become the main focal point on stage. My ego was appeased. David and I were still best friends. It would be a while yet before he became unrecognisable as the friend I grew up with.

The only problem with our third album was perhaps David's vocals, which now suddenly changed. Gone was all the raw rasping breathless intonation of his previous incarnation. He had dropped his vocal style to a lower register. He had begun crooning like Bryan Ferry, a fact not unnoticed by the music press. I believe our third album would have received significantly more critical acclaim had it not been for David's overly mannered vocals. David was the band's figurehead; the press often refused to look beyond him. Musically we were much more innovative than David's rather soulless presentation of us. And yet every penny we made from this album, like the others, went into his pocket. One reviewer spoke of my "rubbery and slippery bass lines" as "deranged" which I liked as a testimony. The single from the album, 'Wonders Seen', reached number fifty-six in the UK charts. Nothing much to shout about, but a great improvement on all our previous efforts in our home country. The *NME* now had to take notice of us and hated us with the same fervour they hated Margaret Thatcher and Ronald Reagan. Our image had by now become more sophisticated. We had all cut our hair shorter. Mine was black and white for a while. I had shaved off my eyebrows and always wore dark shades of lipstick on stage. David was going through his Andy Warhol phase. He was almost supernaturally beautiful to look at in this period. Glasses suited him. We now combined the makeup with smart suits, vintage dress shirts and waistcoats. We stopped wearing women's earrings.

We now began headlining gigs around the UK. We still weren't attracting large audiences, but I began noticing the people at our concerts looked like us and danced and sang along to our songs. Often when we walked offstage there was an elated urge to hug each other. We went back to Japan where the adulation got still crazier. And this was contrasted with the virtual indifference we met with during a short tour of America. We were never to achieve more than a tiny cult following in the US.

It was during this time that I first met Giuliana. She was an Italian dancer studying at the Royal School of Ballet, but her ambition was to dance in Pina Bausch's Tanztheater company. I first saw her on the stairs of a building in South Kensington. She was leaving a party just as I was arriving. For a moment we looked at each other with a kind of burrowing shock of recognition. The sight of her, both intimately familiar and exotically mysterious, I experienced as a kind of coded astrological prediction. Now and again we come across someone who in a moment restores to us all our innocence, who forces us to own the depths of our vulnerability, who will make us climb up higher, reach out further. Giuliana had this effect on me. She had long jet-black Medusa hair, an almost oriental shape to her piercing dark eyes, olive skin and always dressed all in black. She was like the essence of Italy in female form. And Italy was always where I went when I daydreamed. I spent the entire evening asking everyone at the party who she was. No one knew her phone number, only that she was studying ballet at a school in Covent Garden. I began casually wandering around Covent Garden whenever possible. The day I first saw her there I was dressed in a Chinese red army uniform complete with red-badged cap. In hindsight, not the best look. But it did initially make her smile. She loathed all forms of social injustice and uniforms of oppression. With my eyeliner and lipstick offsetting my army attire I was like a protest banner, eloquent in my mockery of martial law. After the brief amusement the impact of my appearance raised, she was chilly with me. She stood looking intensely into my eyes with an intimidating lofty self-command. But I had been reared in coldness and felt myself standing on native ground.

I immediately began learning Italian. I'm a quick learner, as long as I can learn alone, without any witness to the fumbling errors I make along the way.

David at this time had taken against Billy. Increasingly he listened to Billy with an impatient furrowing of his brows. Often

Billy wasn't invited to participate in interviews or even rehearsals sometimes. I should have realised then David was beginning to change. His policing of everything concerning the band was becoming dictatorial. I tried to persuade him out of this hostility towards Billy. But David took any small criticism to heart and brooded on it. He was a very prickly and defensive person. He quickly made me feel my conduct in intervening was an act of betrayal towards him. I dropped the subject. Billy was to be sacrificed. It was the first signs of the emerging tyrant in David, the despotic overlord.

Giuliana agreed to see me now and again, but not very often. All the intimacy we created together she quashed by refusing to see me in the following days. She always brought us back to square one. We went for walks in St James' Park or along the Embankment. We found it easy to talk to each other. Usually in English, sometimes in Italian, when my mistakes would make her laugh. Laughter didn't come easily to her and every time I made her laugh I felt I had hit the jackpot. I liked to hear her talk. When you stop to think about it, it's rare to cherish the act of listening to someone else talk. Her smile, in its full expanse, was almost as radiantly beautiful as David's. I remember one particular conversation we had about London's statues. We both acknowledged it was a terrific stroke of luck to be born British or Italian. Not because of wars won and empires achieved but because of how many fellow countrymen and women we could turn to for inspiration. But very few of the individuals who made me feel lucky to be British were represented by the statues in London. So, instead of the commemorated statesmen, politicians, businessmen, pillars of the establishment, individuals who offered no creative or pioneering inspiration to me, we began to populate the park and its environs with more worthy statues of our own choosing. Nominated by me were Virginia Woolf, Lord Byron and Thomas Tallis; Giuliana opted for Emily Bronte, Margot Fonteyn and Ninette de Valois, the founder of the Royal Ballet.

But despite how much we laughed and mentally danced together, she made a point of continually telling me she wasn't physically attracted to me. I chose not to believe her. One time, sitting on a bench on the South Bank, within sight of all the second-hand book stalls, I noticed a small scar on her foot and caressed it. She shot up as if I had fired an electrical charge into her body. Soon, becoming ever more conscious of how fiercely she withdrew from all physical contact, I developed a theory that she had been abused as a child and was terrified of being touched, terrified of being kissed. That it was the scenario she most feared, but also the scenario she most wanted. I began to convince myself she was setting me the challenge of breaking through her fearful resistance, of taking her forcefully in my arms and kissing her. I had to emulate George Emerson in *A Room with a View*. To make her see me as the prince and not the toad I had to kiss her without her permission. Except she channelled all her resources of icy resistance into intimidating me whenever a moment of physical intimacy loomed. I told myself there are moments in life when the male is called upon to be decisive, assertive. Except I had never had access to that brazen competitive masculine confidence which enables a man to look a woman directly in the eye, pull her towards him through the firm ambitious resolve of his gaze. I began to experience Giuliana's erotic opposition as a seminal personal challenge. Everything that had happened to me with women seemed to highlight some central infirmity in my will, as if it was unable to sprout through the soil into sunlight. No female, beginning with my mother, had ever really held out both her hands to me. As if I couldn't manifest the confidence, the integrity of feeling, to inspire such courage. My head was always too active in matters of the heart. This was my chance to turn the boy into a man.

What I didn't know then and what has since become a conviction is that, as far as I can see, women have a guiding inborn knowledge of the children they are destined to bring into the world and the children themselves can move mountains to get themselves born. And if you are not the requisite father then, no matter how exalted the relationship, no matter how much heart you underwrite, you will be cast off.

I've always loved walking through cities at dawn. The sense it gives you of entering into a new existence with a clean slate. At five in the morning I made my way through Green Park, kicking up dew when I took short-cuts over the grass, past Buckingham Palace, to Victoria station with a light bag slung over my shoulder. From Dover I caught the ferry to Calais. Stood on the deck with the mist and the spray moistening my hair. The surge of the waves throwing me against the rail. I felt I was in my element. I was on my way to pay Giuliana a surprise visit in Italy. I was going to kiss her without her permission, on her native ground. I caught a taxi across Paris and ate lunch on the terrace of a brasserie. I went to the Musée Rodin (an experience of love and wonder I was to recall in detail at least once a week during the following years); I sat in the Jardin de Luxembourg, people watching while I smoked cigarettes. Then I caught the night train from Gare de Lyon to Roma Termini. Those were the good old days when you didn't have to book everything in advance; you could jump aboard the train on a whim without a ticket and pay your fare to the guard. The coffee I had in Rome the next morning was like ambrosia of the gods. I walked to the Forum, a sense of achievement gusting clean bracing air through my thoughts. Then I returned to the station to catch another train. Luckily I had never told Giuliana about my adventure in Kansas City. I was, of course, recycling a compliment. Men though do that all the time. We were recycling compliments long before we were recycling our rubbish.

Soon there were mountains outside the greasy window. The next train I caught was a little diesel train with only two carriages which seemed to belong to a funfair. I took note of the names of the stations we stopped at but couldn't find them on the torn scrap of map I had brought with me. The train wheezed through tunnels and there were fields of sunflowers and maize where women with scarves over their heads busied themselves with baskets. I felt like I was going back in time. Arriving in a still more distant decade at every new station.

In a place called Tizernia I had to wait two hours before the connecting train arrived. I walked around the town. Everyone stared at me with hostility. They seemed to want me to know they were better than me. A stance I always associate with racism, homophobia, misogyny, nationalism. This wasn't the big hearted, generous spirited Italy I was accustomed to. Fame, like being in love, can at times bring with it the conceited (and obnoxious) belief that you are a somebody person in a world of nobody people. I tried to feel that now, to shrink these belligerent people into nobody people. But their unkindness upset me. I couldn't escape it. It was perhaps the first time I seriously considered abandoning my habit of wearing makeup every day, all day.

I caught another fairground train. I had been travelling thirty-six hours. The railway sidings were high with luminous wild flowers in abundance. The stations were all tiny and immaculately kept as if the pride and joy of each uniformed master with his flag and a whistle. This journey lasted two hours. I got off at another small station up in the mountains flanked by broad sweeps of meadowland where cattle grazed. Outside, young boys were playing football in the piazza. By my calculations I was now a couple of bus rides away from the mountain village in the Molise where Giuliana had been born. This however proved untrue. I was told I had to double back on my tracks. I sat on a green bench, lit a cigarette and, surrounded by mountains and lush green slopes, waited for the fairground train to come back. Outside the next station I got off at, there was an empty bus waiting, as if expecting me. I found it hard to understand the dialect of these mountain people, but eventually gathered from the driver that he could take me to a village not far from Giuliana's home. I was the only passenger on the bus. For almost an hour we serpentined our way along high hillside roads. The driver hooted his horn and waved at everyone we passed, workers in fields, solitary figures by the roadside. He even stopped the bus at one point and conducted a fifteen-minute conversation with a man tending sheep.

Eventually we came to the end of the line. I was told the last bus to Giuliana's village had been cancelled and it was an eight-kilometre walk. I didn't mind. The air was bracing, and I relished the prospect of not being cooped up in another bus or train. It was all uphill to begin with. The sun was setting and there was an abundance of wild alpine flowers everywhere. On this lonely mountain road, my small bag slung over my shoulder, I fancied myself a romantic figure, a kind of modern-day Percy Bysshe Shelley. The presence of unadulterated nature, as I stood surveying its expanse, altered the rhythm of my breathing, slowed it down, sent it deeper into my diaphragm. More of me came out on my exhalations as if I was meeting the world with bigger expectations. The cows I passed, swinging their tails and making their bells tinkle, seemed larger than life. I had travelled a long way from the music industry. Sometimes I wished I could name the flowers I passed. I experienced them - their bristling seed heads, dark-veined overlapping petals - as emblems of encouragement. For a moment I was at peace with the world and its wonders. The entire journey had been worth it for this one moment alone.

It quickly became dark and soon the road on either side was flanked by thick forest. I could barely see more than a few feet in front of me. The trees became sentient presences, watchful ancient guardians, neither kind nor cruel. I began to feel light on my feet, dwarfed, as if I was merely something the trees had dreamed into existence. But really, I knew they had no need of me, no need of any human beings. Now and again a car sped past. I wasn't sure if I felt thankful for these reminders of civilisation or affronted by the breach of the pulsing constellated silence they momentarily caused.

An hour later I was still blundering my way through the

clotted darkness when a car pulled up alongside me. A young man with a pony tail asked me if I needed a lift. I accepted, and quickly discovered he was Giuliana's older brother. He didn't have a clue who I was. Clearly Giuliana hadn't spoken about me to her family. He was excited when I told him she had no idea I was coming. I thought I detected a note of cruelty towards his sister in his excitement, as if he knew my unheralded appearance would distress rather than please her and he relished the prospect. For the first time it crossed my mind that my decision to take Giuliana by surprise might be a humiliating error of judgement on my part.

The village was more modern than I expected. I was robbed of some of the anticipated excitement by arriving here with someone to whom it was all commonplace. While walking up the stairs to the second-floor apartment where Giuliana's family lived, I was as nervous as I always was when doing the walk from dressing room to stage. Giuliana though wasn't at home. Only her mother. The first thing she said was to tell me it was forbidden to smoke in the house (I had a lit cigarette). She also made it eloquently clear with facial expressions that she had nothing but scorn for my appearance. After hearing from Giuliana's brother about the difficulties I had had getting there and that Giuliana had no idea I was coming she asked, with barely concealed contempt, why I hadn't phoned. I was jocularly offhand with her. I could say things in Italian I would never say in English. I never felt it mattered what I said in Italian; it was like spending someone else's money. I was surprised when she offered to make me some dinner. Giuliana's brother then left to go and fetch his sister. I was never to see her visceral reaction to my arrival in her village. I had come all this way to take her by surprise and, at the last moment, the script had been changed without my consent. A sore point, generally, for any actor about to deliver his lines. Nevertheless, her startled face when she beheld me in her kitchen was a verification that feeling comes quicker than thought. As ever she refused to belittle herself into the kind of everyday experience I could take for granted. Because perhaps I spent so much time with her in my mind, when I did see her she still seemed soaked in the sacramental properties of my imagination. Giuliana's mother had served me a plate of pasta and feigned surprise that I knew how to eat spaghetti. It was the first thing she said to Giuliana when she entered the kitchen. "Look, he knows how to eat spaghetti." Giuliana appeared both pleased and irritated. I asked about a nearby hotel. This caused the mother some more amusement. "He thinks he's in Rome," she said. Giuliana told me for about the third time that I was mad. *Ma sei pazzo.*

We went out for a walk together after dinner. We had a glass of wine in a trattoria. I caught the eye of a woman at another table. She smiled. She clearly believed me and Giuliana were lovers. Any onlooker would jump to that conclusion. It saddened me that in someone else's mind I was free to touch any part of Giuliana's body I chose. It seemed the reality of my life fell short even of the imagination of strangers.

Afterwards she led me through a dimly lit labyrinth of arches and narrow winding streets to a high vantage point overlooking a canyon of darkness. I knew now was the moment I had to kiss her without her permission. I even thought she was expecting it of me. I've never learned to swim. When I was a little boy I used to fill up a sink and dare myself to put my head under the water. I never could. I felt like that now. That I was being asked to put my head under the water and I couldn't do it. Instead of kissing her I lowered my eyes and, while my body contracted in an agony of knotted shyness, told her I was in love with her. Those words should be a rope thrown up at a window that one is prepared to climb, not another excuse for lowering one's eyes and feeling sorry for oneself. She looked at me as though I had just asked her to follow me along a tightrope over an abyss. Sometimes you wonder how much causality there is in the gestures you imagine but don't perform. Perhaps less than we think.

I stayed there for two nights, sleeping in Giuliana's bed. She had to sleep in her parent's room. They were a poor family, living in a cramped apartment. I got on well with her father despite an unpropitious opening when he told me the Germans had behaved better in the village during the war than the English and advised me not to tell anyone my nationality. Giuliana and I got on as well as we always did, but there was no let-up in her policing of the physical barriers she had constructed between us.

My long journey back to London was a forlorn affair. In common with Monday mornings, return journeys, in my experience, are dispiriting affairs. Like the exiting from a casino of a compulsive gambler who has once again lost more than he has gained. The bounty of anticipation and speculation of the outward journey, all its liquid prospects of prosperity, has withered and hardened into inescapable knowledge. As if you're left with little more than a receipt. On return journeys I was often sobered into taking on the guise of my own accountant. Reassessing my investments, stocktaking my assets. And, as a result, felt myself edged closer to that final reckoning which awaits us all.

When, at the end of the summer, Giuliana returned to London our friendship continued without any significant changes. We saw each other once or twice a week. One night we went to see Pina Bausch's dance company perform. David came too. I was blown away by the beauty of the performance. David and I were recognised in the theatre bar and I could sense Giuliana enjoyed the attention fame grants. She had now left the Royal Ballet Company and joined a modern dance group.

Soon we began rehearsing new material for the next album. David's songwriting prowess had gone up another notch. I loved all the new compositions. We gave more thought to arrangement and harmony. By now we could all take pride in how well we had mastered our respective instruments. Billy wasn't invited to these rehearsals. David's decision. Billy was never formally fired. David didn't like confrontations. It was by now, in incremental degrees, becoming more of an effort to get along with David.

There was a constant strain of compromise on my part involved. He compelled me to shrink in his company. The former hallmark of our friendship of us irresistibly breaking in on what the other was saying, layering in a new depth of communion, was gone. Rarely did we inspire a new idea in each other. More and more I detected a concealed snort of contempt behind his smile, like an outline under a sheet. It was getting to the point where neither of us could make a remark without disturbing the other's equanimity. We had ceased to take as much pleasure in each other's company as in former times. We had perhaps both begun to grow out of the habit of the other's mind. The old sense of fusion which always quickened the time we spent together was in decline. At times I recoiled from what I saw as his vanities when we were in public. I found the way he represented me in his stories and anecdotes increasingly irritating. As if I was little more than a foil to the achievements of the central character in every narrative, which was him. I also noticed his powers of negotiation had improved dramatically in the social sphere. He changed his way of talking to suit the environment and the company. I never now saw him look unsure of himself as he often had in the past, when sometimes he would catch my eye and we would silently communicate our solidarity and affection for each other. The more confidence a person acquires, it sometimes seems to me, the less likeable they become. I liked David better when he was more vulnerable, less sure of himself.

New Romanticism was now beginning to take off as the next British youth movement and we were no longer the only boys to walk London's streets wearing makeup. One night I was taken to the Blitz. Steve Strange at the door and Boy George in the cloakroom. I was never a great fan of nightclubs and soon left.

I began to see less of David outside the commitments of the band. For the first time I wasn't aware of what was happening in his personal life. There were no girlfriends that I knew about. And yet there was a lot of romantic yearning, outstretched hands, in some of the new lyrics he wrote. David rarely showed an obvious sign of preferring any individual woman to all the others. There were even moments when I wondered if he might be a kind of celibate gay. He once told the press he was bisexual, but this was another of his publicity stunt fictions. It was hard to picture him dishevelled, in the throes of physical passion, but then the same has been said of me.

Also, the four of us together were an intimidating presence. Individually we were all standoffish. As a unit we put out a repelling forcefield. The intimacy we shared as a band was not dissimilar to the makeup we wore in its intent and effect of keeping the world at arm's length. It wasn't easy for outsiders to enter our atmosphere. It required a lot of self-assurance and courage. Groupies managed it, because they were driven by a blinding and single-minded determination. But very few women who saw us as more than sex objects. I suppose this might suggest an absence of generosity in us. But, unlike David, I did at least try to talk to the people who found the courage to approach us.

When we began to record the next album we had several disagreements in the studio. Usually about the clarinet and saxophone parts I was contributing to certain songs. Then there was another song on which David wanted no bass or drums at all. Now and again I detected a new undertow of hostility in David towards me. He was much more argumentative. I began to realise we were no longer best friends. I was closer to Pete now. David had begun hanging out with people I didn't know. It upset me.

Our single 'The Way of Our Fathers' entered the top thirty and we did *Top of the Pops* for the first time. It should have been a high point in our career. Appearing on the TV show we had watched in awe as kids. But David was especially unapproachable that day and I was upset by his chilled aloofness. The dressing room before we went out to mime was an oppressive and icy place. I tried to lighten the mood, but it was like he now saw me as a hired hand who was best ignored.

The new album far outsold all our previous records. We were

now about to embark on a world tour, beginning in the UK, concluding with two nights at Hammersmith Odeon.

On the eve of the tour David organised a meeting and announced he couldn't go through with it unless we changed the set design – which he had mostly designed himself. It was too late to create a new set design which had already been constructed. All the tickets had been sold; every venue was a sell-out. I knew David hated touring. He had always hated it. And it wasn't the first time he had turned himself into a petulant diva on the eve of a tour. But, this time, I lost my temper with him. I told him I had had enough of his megalomania. I told him that it was as much my band as his and I was sick of him implementing all the laws. He seemed wholly prepared for my outburst, as if he had scripted the entire confrontation. He told us he thought the band had run its course and the time had come to go our separate ways. Pete and Alan were no less stunned than I was. A good thing about arguments is you sometimes hear revelatory observations about yourself that are otherwise kept private. I thought maybe David would provide one of these now. But I simply found out he didn't much care for my company anymore. I looked at him and felt the full force of our estrangement. Once upon a time he had almost seemed like an extension, a fantastic conjuring trick, of my own imagination. Now he had strayed far from my jurisdiction. His volition was like a foreign language of which I had no knowledge. He made me feel the past, our entire history together, was something illegal that I was trying to smuggle through customs. Together we had created the world we lived in, exported it out into worldwide realms of reality and there was no denying it was an admirable shared achievement; now he had suddenly vacated that world, scorched it to extinction.

"We'll do this last tour and then call it a day," he said. He then checked his watch. Something I had rarely seen him do. In fact, I couldn't remember him ever wearing a watch. It was like he was letting us know he now had a more important life somewhere else. He told us we wouldn't announce the split until the end of the tour. The next night we performed two songs on the *Old Grey Whistle Test*. Not surprisingly we all looked shellshocked, like showroom dummies, bereft of an inner life. Just as there are few experiences more exhilarating than playing a great concert, there are few more depressing than performing when your heart's not in it. A week later David appeared alone on *Riverside*, a BBC music show, and announced that, by mutual consent, the band was splitting up after what would now be our farewell tour. On the show he played two of our songs on acoustic guitar. As if to demonstrate how little he needed us. I have to admit they were both very moving and he had never looked so beautiful or conducted himself with such charismatic self-confidence.

It was a couple of days later that Giuliana asked to see me. We met outside the British Film Institute on the Embankment and she told me she was moving in with David. I was speechless. I felt as though the tape on which my life was recorded had snapped. The two shredded ends whirling around on different spools, forever now separated. It was true I had noticed once or twice that she and David were shy with each other, but I had no inkling they ever saw each other except when she was with me. There was never, to my eyes, any outward sign they especially enjoyed each other's company. Clearly though they had done a great job at hoodwinking me. I couldn't help imagining both the pangs of conscience and the conspiratorial laughter they might have shared. They had turned me into an object of pity and mirth. *Poor old Nick.* I'd always prided myself on being a sharply perceptive person, sensitive to nuances of feeling in those close to me. I now had to downgrade this obviously erroneous high evaluation of my mind-reading skills.

I got up and walked away. I didn't want to hear her apologies. They were for her benefit, not mine. I had always believed I knew Giuliana well. It was an achievement I took pride in. If someone were to write her biography my contribution, I'd always felt, would be invaluable. I had spent a lot of time and energy thinking about her. My ideas were all at sea now, bobbing about on the surface and menaced by a synchronised circle of fins. The humiliation burrowed deeper when I realised how comprehensively I had deluded myself. She wasn't pathologically repelled by physical tenderness at all; she was simply telling the truth: I held no physical attraction for her at all.

The next day I left her a package. It contained all the clothes I had been wearing at our final meeting. Even my shoes. Even my boxers. I included no accompanying note. Why do we men always want women to see the pain they cause us? We do, don't we? That's why I left Giuliana my clothes in a brown paper parcel. We always want women to feel on our behalf. Because when we understand they will continue to laugh and dance without any diminishment of heart after we disappear our world caves in. We can't just go away and weep in private though. First of all we have to dramatise our hurt. We have to pour forth our pleas of please and sorry and how dare you. We might start off by standing under our jilter's window in the rain (we like it that it's raining, the rain gives every entreaty we call up a more impassioned touch of theatre.) And despite the hurt, the churning hollow wretchedness, we're also secretly pleased with ourselves beneath the window. We have a soft spot for the heartbroken supplication. It's the impetus that gets poetry written, religions underway.

David and I could barely look at each other throughout the tour. We had separate dressing rooms, travelled in different cars, stayed in different hotels. The animosity between us was so palpable it often caused embarrassment among the road crew, the sound engineer and tour manager at soundchecks. Every glance I shot at him was dipped in venom. Pete and Alan weren't overly fond of him either. David cut an isolated figure but with no lessening of the obstinacy with which he pursued his own aims. The Japanese session musician he had hired to play guitar on the tour, a new friend of his, was his ally. And Giuliana, who often came to the gigs. A sign the two of them gave no thought whatsoever to my feelings.

But here we were every night playing all the songs that contained the sap and juice of our deep friendship. I never realised until moments on that tour how potently a song can preserve and convey significance from the past. The nostalgic emotion music kindles runs much deeper, produces more detail than anything a photograph can evoke. I began to understand it was emotion rather than time that charted the continuity of a life. I remember once reading about protons and how they leap about without ever occupying intervening space. I see a wisdom in that. When there is no emotion, time stops happening and leaves in its wake little more than an intervening space. The continuity of my life was charted by so many emotions I had shared with David that without him it seemed like I would be left with nothing but intervening space. I couldn't believe our legacy together was something he didn't feel the need to protect at all costs. Later, during the British leg of the tour, I even made tentative overtures to make it up with him. As I said, Giuliana would often attend those gigs. One night I asked to speak to her. I told her she and David had my blessing. She was nice to me and I found I was able to like her again. But there was no yielding on David's part. His mind was made up. It was like he had begun forgetting me even while I played music with him on the same stage.

During the tour I found out my father was dying. On a day off I visited him. I was aware of still appearing an irresponsible teenage boy at heart when I walked into his room at the hospice. I was wearing eyeliner and a woman's full-length tweed coat I had found in a charity shop. I was an eloquent portrait of how my father thought I lived which caused him, in about equal measure, both embarrassment and pride.

My mother told me to give my father a kiss. Clumsily I went for his far cheek and knocked him off his high bank of pillows. He groaned and looked flustered. Then he hid his discomfort as he was so apt to do throughout his life. Muted alarms kept going off in other rooms. My father's alarm button was clipped to the blanket. His emaciated hand hovered near it. A television hung suspended from a metal brace half way up the wall. The blank screen reflected him back to himself. I wondered what that would be like later when we had gone and, alone, he looked up at the reflection of his dying body. How vast the universe would seem and yet how intimately he would feel its breath on his body. Impending death made him seem like a saint. He was profound and wise lying there – attributes he had never attained in life. Now and again a sad apologetic smile appeared on his face when he remembered me and glanced in my direction. He probably thought I was bored. As a child I had never done much to hide the boredom my parents induced in me. He had always been oddly sympathetic in this regard, as if the house in which we lived and all its monotonously reiterated routines bored him too. I tried to imagine myself in his predicament. I asked myself what might possibly bring me comfort if I was consigned to a room I would never leave. It would be music, of course. Music makes you feel younger, more confident you can take on the world and the obstacles it throws at you. Music can be the medium of sharing experience in a purified and heightened form; but it can also make being alone a stirring and highly privileged place to be. Music was the air I breathed.

I asked him if he was frightened. He didn't answer but looked at me with a hint of irritation. I immediately regretted it. It seemed a selfish question on my part. Afterwards it occurred to me that this was the only time in my life I had asked him about his feelings. He had difficulty speaking. He lifted his hand. I flinched in my chair at the bedside. He put his hand down. Had he meant me to take it? The sad apologetic smile appeared again. I could tell it cost him a lot to look at me. I represented next month, next year, everything he would never know again. Even in death he seemed to think of himself as a burden. Before leaving I said, almost under my breath, "Dad." The effect it had was like the tolling of an old bell - broadening circles of silence seemed to follow in its wake and gather the world inside my head to attention.

I was upset David didn't fly back with me from France to attend the funeral.

One of the gigs we did at Hammersmith Odeon was filmed and recorded for a live album and video. You can see many of the clips on YouTube. When I saw the footage I was amazed with how much confident aplomb I enacted my onstage persona. Because inside I was a heartbroken man. Though some of our most devoted fans apparently detected something was wrong between me and David.

After the tour was over, Giuliana fulfilled her ambition and joined Pina Bausch's Tanztheater company and David moved to Germany with her. He recorded his first solo album there, using Pete on some of the tracks, which left me feeling betrayed by Pete too. I never saw David again. He and Giuliana eventually got married. And then divorced. They had a son together.

David didn't enjoy being a popstar. He believed he had much more to offer. And he was right about that. But so too did we other members of Orfée have more to offer. No doubt he justifies his decision to break up the band with the conviction that his solo albums were more mature and worthy of critical acclaim than our albums as a band. But this isn't true. Orfée were and still are underrated because, initially, we made our mistakes in public and afterwards were associated with the New Romantic movement and its derided apolitical decadent ethos. There are two excellent songs on David's first album, both of which could have been Orfée songs and arranged better. His second album was largely a dull uninspired affair only redeemed by the great improvement in his lyric writing. He had discovered a talent for making poetic drama of personal experience. Many of his lyrics sounded like prayers. Finally, he was baring his soul to the world. But no one can tell me that, as a band, we wouldn't have come up with something much more compelling and praiseworthy than his first two solo albums. It wasn't until his third album, eight years later, that he found his voice as a solo artist. I still to this day believe David broke us up before we had reached the peak of our creative powers as a collective entity.

I can't now remember much about the year following the demise of the band. I raged against David to anyone who would listen. Including one journalist who published a sensationalised version of my story in which David featured as a megalomaniacal monster. I knew he'd never speak to me again after the contemptuous mauling I publicly gave him. One day, remembering Rodin, I bought a bag of clay, and from then onwards sculpted grotesque human forms deep into the night when I couldn't sleep. These figures became my friends. Otherwise I now began to live in the past, something of which I had no previous experience. Rarely was I reconciled to the time present world. I can't remember how exactly I met Linda the year after. But London now felt to me like a film in which I had only an insignificant role. It made me feel, with all its associations and reminders, that I had become a ghost of myself, forever fated to dwell in the regret of all I had lost. I knew if I wanted to get out of my head and live in my body again I had to leave London. For me it had always been Italy that offered the greatest promise of physical wellbeing. I went to Florence to study classical sculpture. I finally stopped wearing makeup. For the next ten years or so I survived on session work. I was in demand for a while. Then, as if overnight, the world forgot about me.

8

All day at work I had been impatient to return to Bysshe. Her bounding floundering syncopations were present as a ghostly force in my own limbs. The world I saw through the windscreen of my delivery van sometimes threatened to take on the digitalised and acrylic properties of Bysshe's world. Faced with customers, the instinct of my hands was to look for a keyboard to type out my dialogue. I was disappointed I couldn't right click on their profile to see what groups they belonged to. I felt estranged from my own body, rather as I had when on stage, except I was missing the euphoria.

I was also struck by the facade of normality constructed on every household I entered. I found I was less believing of it. I felt I now had a more informed idea of what might lurk beneath the painted and lacquered surface, a more informed idea of what people got up to in secret.

As soon as Bysshe appeared on the screen, my little minx of an accomplice, I felt a warm glow of affection for her. It occurred to me that I probably liked Bysshe more than I liked myself. I was a bit sick of my immaturity, my laissez-faire default setting, my failure to inspire confidence or provide any sense of security. Bysshe, unlike me, did not withdraw from intimacy; she was more trusting and as a result, it seemed to me, more successful in dramatising identity. She even had better friends than I did.

She was still standing by Nomedo's fowl coups. She had befriended Nomedo last night so he would always now know when she was online. In fact, an instant message arrived from him almost immediately.

IM: Nomedo Arumi: Greetings girl. Where are you?

IM: Bysshe Artaud: Standing by your fowl coups, master.

IM: Nomedo Arumi: If you're willing to submit to me it must be now.

IM: Bysshe Artaud: Can I just have three minutes, master?

IM: Nomedo Arumi: Come NOW girl.

I realised I was genuinely apprehensive about this business of relinquishing my freedom. There was a suspicion rooted in me, heavy and glutinous, that it was something that was going to affect the way I related to myself in real life.

Bysshe joined Nomedo in the town's market square. He led her into a barren room where I noticed some worrying pose balls scattered about – *rape the slut*, *double trouble*, *suck it*, *kneel*, *knees up* and *sleep*. Nomedo was bare-chested tonight, his muscles flexed, with a serpent tattoo on his athletic chest. When I zoomed in on him, he stared back at me with blinking soulless blue eyes. Behind him knelt the slave girl, Tala Aslan.

"Are you ready to submit?"

What choice did I have if I wanted to legalise Bysshe in this world which somewhere hid my daughter and not be deported as an illegal immigrant?

"Yes master," said Bysshe.

"Take off your clothes girl."

Bysshe displayed her naked body to what I felt was an intense critical scrutiny. There was a long silence. I wondered if Nomedo was having second thoughts. Perhaps he didn't find Bysshe sufficiently attractive without her clothes? I saw her from behind. She didn't have an ounce of fat or a filament of cellulite on her body. She looked like a long-legged nubile nineteen-year-old. Wasn't that exactly what the modern world, aesthetically, demanded of women?

A series of blue folders finally appeared on the top right corner of my screen. Nomedo Arumi gave Bysshe a windfall of items – a lavish flexi silk top (sultry sex foil), skirt, right and left armband, Nadu animation, a metallic collar, slave ownership papers, a library of sex and slave animations among other things.

"Put all these things on, girl."

I went to my inventory and right clicked on each item. Fluttering red silk ribbons magically attached themselves to Bysshe's naked form, a collar appeared around her neck and typescript above her head now announced to the world that she was Nomedo's kajira. Then she fell beautifully to her knees. This was the moment I had waited for. Bysshe had acquired grace. I now wanted to follow Nomedo all around the city. To see her perform the slave geisha walk and then drop to her knees every time her master stopped in his tracks. I read the document that appeared on the screen – *This document confirms the beast known as Bysshe Artaud is owned by the First Sword of Argentum, known as Nomedo Arumi.*

There was then some kind of ritual with the collar. I was required to type Nomedo's name together with some symbols into my computer. He spoke of programming commands into the metal collar and I did for a moment wonder how much of her autonomy Bysshe was about to lose.

Crimson Daggers =CD= Slave (slim): Bysshe Artaud has a new owner, Nomedo Arumi.

Crimson Daggers =CD= Slave (slim): Bysshe Artaud's collar is locked in place.

Crimson Daggers =CD= Slave (slim): Leash length set to 2 meters.

I received a message announcing Nomedo would immediately be notified if Bysshe removed the collar.

"Now follow me, girl," he said.

Nomedo led Bysshe out of the room and across the city square. The slave girl followed us. Several times I was able to marvel at the spectacle of Bysshe falling adoringly to her knees. Nomedo now had some control of her animations. More second thoughts arrived. I worried about the consequences this theft of her autonomy might have when, if, I met Katie.

Bysshe followed him into a bleak brick building where there was a furnace and an anvil.

"Lie down on the table, girl."

I clicked on a poseball and Bysshe obediently stretched herself out on the rack.

Nomedo Arumi grabs the girl roughly and ties her arms and legs to the table.

Nomedo Arumi examines her left thigh.

Nomedo Arumi puts on a pair of heavy gloves.

Nomedo Arumi withdraws from the fire a white hot branding iron.

Nomedo Arumi aims the iron at the girl's thigh.

Nomedo Arumi presses firmly.

Tala Aslan closes her eyes remembering her own pain....

IM Nomedo Arumi: You can cry out in pain, Bysshe.

I had forgotten I was supposed to roleplay.

Bysshe Artaud has done her best to stifle a scream of agony, but now it emerges on a high shrill blood-curdling note.

Nomedo Arumi watches the flesh sizzle and burn.

Nomedo Arumi withdraws the branding iron.

Nomedo Arumi places the iron back into the fire.

Nomedo Arumi admires his branding.

Nomedo Arumi: It's a fine brand.

Bysshe Artaud: Thank you, master.

Nomedo Arumi: You are now collared and branded as mine, girl.

Bysshe Artaud: It is indeed a fine brand, master.

Nomedo Arumi unties the girl from the table.

Not of her own volition, Bysshe immediately knelt down at her master's feet. There was now a black hieroglyph on her thigh.

Nomedo Arumi: ((Have to log for ½ hour))

Tala Aslan: ((We will await your return with eagerness, master))

Tala could speak for herself. I was hoping for Bysshe's sake and my own that Nomedo's power supply would be short circuited by a calamitous thunderstorm in the next half an hour or that he would suddenly go down with dual-motion food poisoning.

"I think I'll explore my new home a bit," said Bysshe from her geisha kneeling position.

Tala Aslan: Ok sis. I'll prepare master's evening meal. Just let me know if you need any help with anything.

I turned Bysshe round to face me. Her expression seemed less glazed, more alert to the inspirations of intelligence. Her new garments had added an additional depth of mischief to her character.

Off we went together through the grim dark-age streets of Argentum. She was compelled by law to kneel in front of any male she met and greet him as master. This happened once as she made her way alongside a river. I imagined her heart pounding in her chest as she entered a building and ran up some stairs. Nothing but empty rooms. She then shuffled down the cobbled streets towards a civic building. Under a portico was a cage and crouched inside the cage was Alaya Twine. The molecular signalling in my brain was like a scuffle between riot police and protestors as the realisation fought through militant disbelief that this little blonde naked animation inside a cage was my first ever sight of my daughter. I zoomed in on her avatar. She was a skinny beautiful thing with a big wet mouth and a tumult of wavy blonde hair. There was now a kind of Ouija board tension, or so it seemed to me, as the two girls silently studied each other. I waited for the sound of faint hollow rapping which announces an avatar is about to speak. I didn't have to wait long.

Alaya Twine: Come closer, girl.

'Come closer, girl' - the first thing my daughter had ever said to me. I bet no father in the entire history of the world has heard those words from his daughter.

Alaya Twine reaches a hand through the bars.

Bysshe Artaud takes the hand and caresses it, feeling the heat of the female's blood become part of her own warmth and wellbeing. She finds herself trying to picture the child this girl once was.

Don't freak her out, I reprimanded myself. But a terrific

unexpected wave of sadness had swept through me as, for the first time in my life, I experienced myself as a dad, a dad who hadn't been around to watch and help his child grow up. I would have made up stories for her, I would have taught her to sculpt with clay, I would have run across lawns with her on my shoulder, I would have marvelled at her every attempt to achieve identity.

Alaya Twine: Will you help me, girl?

Bysshe Artaud: If I help you escape you have to promise to take me with you and always do your best to see my point of view.

Alaya Twine: You want to run away?

Bysshe Artaud: I want to run away with you. I think we'll make a good team. But I've only got about fifteen minutes before my master returns.

Alaya Twine: Ok. I will take you with me. My name is Alaya.

Bysshe Artaud: Bysshe.

Alaya Twine: Go and find some kind of sharp object you can cut these ropes with. And a pin – a piece of metal I can use to pick the lock of this cage. And also get me some FW clothes.

Bysshe Artaud: FW?

Alaya Twine: Free woman. A long gown, a veil and some boots. ((You don't have to literally get them. Just rp it. I've got all the stuff in my inventory))

Alaya Twine: ((I'll need to disguise myself to get out of this city. Go inside that building there, the infirmary, and rp finding a bundle of old clothes))

Bysshe did as she was told. It brought an incredulous exalted grin to my face that I was talking to my daughter. I felt like I had climbed a high hill and was standing on the summit, the wind gusting ripples out of my clothes and blowing tears into my eyes. Shouldn't I though tell her who I was? The knowledge I was tricking her dirtied my hands. Now and again I felt this unclean-liness sully my mood. At the same time I couldn't conceive of any suitable way of transitioning from the madcap roleplaying world of Bysshe and Alaya to the still more outlandish drama now playing out in real life. My heart was beating too fast, as if I were trespassing on forbidden land, as I sometimes did as a child, as we all sometimes do as children.

I walked Bysshe over to the infirmary. I right clicked on the door to open it. The door spoke to me -

Door: Sorry Bysshe Artaud, this door is locked.

Bysshe Artaud rattles the handle of the door.

Door: Sorry Bysshe Artaud, this door is locked.

Bysshe Artaud charges at the door with her shoulder. The impact of the unyielding heavy oak sends her tumbling backwards onto the paving stones. She falls on her bottom.

Door: Sorry Bysshe Artaud, this door is locked.

Alaya Twine giggles.

I could sense I had made Katie smile in real life. I glowed with physical wellbeing. I pictured her with that smile on her face at her keyboard in a mysterious house all of whose doors, like the one Bysshe couldn't open, were presently locked to me.

Alaya Twine: Try the blacksmith's around the corner. ((And don't forget to rp it all. I'll have to send my captor a notecard showing him my escape was valid))

Bysshe Artaud scurries off to the blacksmith's yard. She picks up a sharp piece of flint she sees on the cobbles, looks around for the other things Alaya requested. Her eyes light up as she spies a black cloak hanging on a hook. She slings that over her arm. A pin, a pin, she says to herself, my kingdom for a pin.

Alaya Twine continues to work at the ropes binding her hands, chaffing her wrists against each other to work the bindings loose.

Bysshe Artaud looks to the heavens in gratitude as she finds a tiny piece of metal by the anvil. She hears harsh raucous male voices in the distance and looks around anxiously for some more clothes.

Alaya Twine beckons to the girl to return now with what she has.

Bysshe Artaud returns to the cage with her haul.

Alaya Twine edges closer to the bars of the cage and swivels around on her haunches so the girl can cut through her ropes.

Bysshe Artaud works the flint back and forth against the rope, biting her lip with concentration.

Alaya Twine feels her heart thump against her chest as she strains her ears for any approaching footsteps.

Bysshe Artaud looks with satisfaction at the frayed rope which is about to snap.

Alaya Twine: ((Click on the rope to bring up the menu))

GMBindings2.3-female(pelvis): Bysshe Artaud finishes cutting Alaya Twine loose allowing her to escape.

Alaya Twine: Hand me the pin quick.

Bysshe Artaud passes Alaya the small bit of metal through the bars.

Alaya Twine inserts the piece of metal into the lock and biting down on her bottom lip turns it this way and that trying to get it to catch in the spring.

Bysshe Artaud squeezes her hands together anxiously as she watches Alaya trying to unlock the cage door.

Alaya Twine, her hand trembling a little with frustration, continues wiggling the metal inside the lock. Finally she succeeds in nestling the piece of metal in exactly the right spot and slowly twists it in the lock, praying it won't snap.

Bysshe Artaud holds her breath.

Alaya Twine listens with relief to the click as the lock is prised open.

The door of the cage swung open and Alaya scurried out.

I had helped my daughter liberate herself from a cage. If only I might someday be able to achieve the same feat, metaphorically, in real life.

I then saw a message at the bottom of my screen announcing Nomedo Arumi was back online. I stiffened in my chair and a muscle screwed itself into a nugget at the back of my neck.

Alaya Twine takes the cloak from Bysshe and quickly puts it on, holding it tight around her nakedness.

IM: Nomedo Arumi: Come to the tavern, girl.

Bysshe Artaud: My master is calling me.

Alaya Twine: You sure you want to escape?

Bysshe Artaud nods.

Alaya Twine: What's his name?

I told her.

Alaya Twine: He's the male who captured me. He was full-on nasty. He started raping me until I showed him I had no rape in my rp limits. I was raped once. Never again. He's 55 m away.

Bysshe Artaud: How do you know that?

Alaya Twine: radar hud.

I received a folder from Alaya called Panther Kit. Inside, apart from a radar hub, was a whip, several bandages, a grapple hook, lots of clothes, some trading items, a canoe and, mysteriously, a "furring rug". Bysshe asked Alaya what a furring rug was.

IM: Alaya Twine: Heavens, you're an innocent! Cybersex. It has lots of sex animations in it. You rez it.

I enjoyed being called an innocent by my daughter. I felt I would like her to feel that to some degree if we met in real life. As a rule I didn't warm to men who never seemed to succumb to doubt - it didn't matter in what cause they advanced their smug assurance.

IM: Nomedo Arumi: Girl. I do not expect to be kept waiting when I call you.

Nomedo Arumi was beginning to give me the creeps. He didn't seem to possess a sense of fun. When Alaya told me he had raped her, anger quivered in my nostrils. I lit a cigarette. This was all suddenly much more of an adrenalin rush than anything I had experienced in real life since walking out on stage. I was fleeing from a tyrant with my daughter. My body was firing up an electrical stormwind of chemicals as if this was something that had to be got through physically.

Alaya Twine: We need to get up on the battlements. Follow me.

I couldn't however move Bysshe. She was down on all fours

wriggling her bottom back and forth. She looked rather comical and I might have laughed had I not been so spooked out by the possibility of Nomedo Arumi getting his hands on her and at the same time of losing track of Katie. I sent her an instant message announcing I was stuck.

IM: Alaya Twine: You wearing a scripted collar?

IM: Bysshe Artaud: What's that?

IM: Alaya Twine: Your collar probably has commands in it your master can control. If so he's probably locked you into place. He might even be able to make you go to him. Have to get that collar off you, girl. Hang on. I'll come back. We have to rp it.

Alaya Twine reappeared and then ambled with a sexy hip swaying walk off to the blacksmith's. She returned holding some cumbersome object in her hand. Bysshe asked what it was.

Alaya Twine: Red hot branding iron.

Bysshe Artaud recoils in alarm.

Bysshe Artaud: You can't use that. The metal will melt into my neck.

Alaya Twine nods. The thing clatters on the cobbles as she throws it away.

IM: Nomedo Arumi: Are you enjoying your punishment, girl?

Alaya Twine kneels down by the side of Bysshe and tries to pick the lock of her collar with the same pin she used to get out of the cage.

I thought I had better buy some time with Nomedo.

IM: Bysshe Artaud: This girl begs forgiveness, master. This girl was preparing a surprise for her master. However she is now frozen with fear and cannot complete her task.

Alaya Twine gently twists the pin of metal to the right and left of the steel collar's lock.

IM: Nomedo Arumi: lol. I will release you now, girl. I want you here at the tavern immediately.

IM: Bysshe Artaud: Yes, master. Thank you, master.

Alaya Twine feels the little shaft give way in the collar as it makes a pinging sound.

Alaya Twine: ((Go to your inventory, right click on the collar and select detach. The minute you do that he will be notified and might come after you so we need to run. CTRL+R))

Bysshe Artaud: Okay.

I removed the collar around Bysshe's neck and set her in motion behind Alaya. She climbed a succession of stairways until she was standing on the battlements.

Alaya Twine: Can you swim? ((swim ao?))

Bysshe had to confess she couldn't swim. An ao is an animation override, a script which replaces the standard movements of your avatar. I was beginning to gain some command of the language of this place.

Alaya Twine: We have to jump. I'll hold you up in the water.

Bysshe Artaud feels her legs sag with fear as she looks down at the distant water.

Alaya Twine: On three. One...Two...Jump!

Bysshe plummeted from the high wall and sank to the bottom of the water in a jiffy. I was informed she was drowning and on top of that had suffered 18% fall damage. There was no sign of Alaya Twine.

Bysshe Artaud clasps the root of a shrub and hauls herself out of the flow of the river onto the grass bank. She crumples to the ground, feeling like a flower that has withered on its stem. She wipes the river muck from her face, shakes the water from her hair and feels the long grass tickling her bare back and legs.

Alaya Twine: ((Hey, good rp hun!))

Bysshe Artaud: ((Thanks))

Bysshe and Alaya made it to a wooden landing stage where a boat waited. It's virtually impossible to walk your avatar and type at the same time so I had not been able to chat with Katie during our escape. Did I feel guilty that I was deceiving her? I did, but I wasn't prepared for how heavily invested she would be in this roleplaying malarkey. There seemed no place for real life in this crazy world. I had to continually justify my undercover espionage though. I told myself I was biding my time. When the appropriate moment arrived, I would bare my soul. And anyway, I argued, deception was often simply a more imaginative mischievous way to get at the truth. Everyone tells lies to get what they want. First of all we tell lies to ourselves and then we tell them to everyone else. That's what the past becomes – a kind of flower bed in which you're uprooting and replanting all the time.

Bysshe was now receiving furious instant messages from her ex-master. I told him that Alaya had forced me at knife-point to help her escape. He demanded to know how she had got hold of a knife seeing as he himself had stripped and searched her for hidden weapons. Bysshe had to admit she had found the female beguiling and had passed her a sharp piece of flint through the bars. He demanded a notecard of all my roleplaying by the cage. He said he doubted the validity of our escape and had had enough of Disney rpers wasting his time. To be called Disney, I already knew, was the most damning insult you could receive in the roleplaying world of Gor. After reading my log of the escape, Nomedo told me he was now not going to rest until he had hunted me and Alaya down. I didn't understand why he was so angry. We had given him a good story to develop. Hunting us down would surely provide an exciting structure for his forthcoming adventures in this world.

"Great!" wrote Katie when I told her. "Another stalker. Just what I need."

"What do you mean?" asked Bysshe.

Alaya Twine tugs a crumpled scroll from her boot and hands it to Bysshe.

I thought better of reminding her she wasn't wearing any boots.

Bysshe received a notecard from Alaya -

Bounty Hunters of Gor. $10,000 offered for Alaya Twine. She is to endure at least 1 hour of extreme torture and humiliation, be enslaved and then sold at auction.

Alaya Twine: Guess someone doesn't like me.

Bysshe Artaud: Someone is paying to have you tortured?

Alaya Twine: Yep.

Bysshe Artaud: You don't know who it is?

Alaya Twine: No idea. Someone I've upset I guess. Me and Zo can be a bit mischievous.

Bysshe Artaud: Zo?

Alaya Twine: Zo is the love of my life. We're inseparable. We're going to get married.

Bysshe Artaud: In here you mean?

Alaya Twine: Yep. We've just met in RL too. You'll meet her. She's being sold at a slave auction later. She might be a bit jealous of you initially. Give her some slack.

So my daughter was attracted to other women. What did I think about that? In a sense all women are attracted to other women. They are constantly fascinated by each other. Women notice the things about each other they want noticed. They see the parts of each other they try to hide. Males can rarely be trusted to be so interested, so perceptive. Just as me and David were more fascinated by each other than by any member of the opposite sex for a long time.

Bysshe Artaud: You've met in real life?

Alaya Twine: Yes, but I don't talk about RL until I know someone well.

Bysshe Artaud: Makes sense.

Alaya Twine: Why don't you join our tribe, Bysshe? We're called the Sa'i Tor Varra. You can either be a cub (a trainee panther) or a camp slave girl.

Bysshe embraced the offer and opted for the cub option. Alaya offered to go shopping with her for all the things she would need. We visited about five shopping malls together and I treated Bysshe to everything Alaya told me she would need for her new life – a bow and arrows, two tomahawks, a dagger, a spear, a whip, two new outfits, new hair, some bracelets, a swim animation overrider and a sexy panther-neko animation overrider. I also treated Alaya to a skimpy new skirt. The first gift I had ever made my daughter. This little lot cost me in the region of 5,000 linden dollars – which I was relieved to work out was only about twenty quid. Bysshe could now crawl on all fours, swing her hips seductively as she walked, swim an elegant breaststroke, fold her arms, rub one foot against the other, lick her wrist and even perform a playful handstand.

"You look great!" Alaya told her when I dressed Bysshe up in her new outfit. She was virtually naked save for little shreds of fur and feathers around her waist, a flimsy black bra and a pair of white fur boots. She had long wild black hair. It felt good to be once again receiving compliments on my appearance, something that hadn't happened to me for years.

"I'll take you back to camp and you can meet my sisters."

Bysshe and Alaya were walking side by side in wild woodlands flanked on either side by steep snow-clad ridges when I heard a high heartbeat gasp of pain from my speakers and was informed that Bysshe had been hit by an arrow -

Gorean Meter 2.6: Anjar Zimmer hit you with arrow long (15%) - strike type: arrow

Alaya Twine: Male intruder.

Bysshe was hit by another arrow and then another. Each time she let out a few rasping notes of discomfort. I watched with some alarm her health diminish on the hud at the top of my screen. I was so nervously affronted by this attack that I became jittery and got in a muddle following the commands of how to use Bysshe's bow. I went into mouselook as I had been told but couldn't for the life of me see Bysshe's assailant who was still hitting her with arrows. She ended up falling in a stream and lost some more of her health. Alaya meanwhile had gone charging off. I could see her, doing a fleet-footed kind of wardance as she shot off a barrage of arrows, chasing the male.

Gorean Meter 2.6 shouts: Alaya Twine has captured Anjar Zimmer.

The blonde male was paralysed inside a gossamer red bubble. I quickly typed some roleplay, eager again to impress my daughter.

Bysshe Artaud wades across the stream towards the male who attacked her. He lies bloodied and muddied in the tall grass. Resting her foot on his shoulder, she grimaces and tugs out the arrow embedded in his flesh. She studies it, satisfies herself it can be used again and puts it in her quiver. A growing red stain, she notices, spreads over the prostrate male's tunic.

Alaya Twine nudges the male with her foot. "Didn't come out of that too well, did you?"

Anjar Zimmer look up at the two beautiful huntresses. He try to stand but too weak.

Alaya Twine: Take his weapons, strip him and search him, sis.

Bysshe Artaud kicks away his bow and takes the knife from his belt. She sees his mouth twitch and wonders if he's going to speak. She crouches down on the grass bank, lifts up his chin and looks him in the eye. "Are you in pain?"

Anjar Zimmer feel her small fingers on his face. "Very pain."

Alaya Twine rips his shirt apart down the middle, exposing his tanned and scarred torso.

Anjar Zimmer: ((I love hard humiliation))

Bysshe Artaud crouches down on her haunches by his feet. She takes the soft leather boot firmly between both hands and yanks, her eyes bright with concentration. She tugs hard, pulling hard at the footwear with her tongue poking out of her mouth.

Alaya Twine cracks her longer fingers and feels inch by inch up the male's breaches, her tongue out as she probes.

Anjar Zimmer close his eyes and feel hands all on his body.

Alaya Twine: Nothing there.

Anjar Zimmer: ((I accept every humiliation))

Alaya Twine takes the whip from her belt and bites the leather straps with her white teeth. She flicks it through the air as a warning.

Anjar Zimmer was now lying on his back naked. Out of curiosity I clicked on his outlandishly large erect member. A menu came up on my screen - *You are playing with Anjar's cock. What would you like to do? Stroke light, Cup balls, Grind, Kick, Slap, Kiss, Lick, Nibble, Grab, Stroke hard, Squeeze balls, Suck.* I chose the *kick* option. That though was a mistake as I then got a quickfire flurry of instant messages from him.

IM: Anjar Zimmer: I love female feet.

IM: Anjar Zimmer: Force me to lick and sniff your feet.

IM: Anjar Zimmer: humiliate me, please.

Alaya Twine stands with her legs braced and raises the whip high. "Hold him still a minute, Bysshe."

I imagined me and Katie laughing together one day in the future at the recollection of this shared adventure.

Alaya Twine feels the familiar demon possess her as she stands with her legs apart wielding the whip. Heat rises to her cheeks. Her hand begins to tremble with guilty excitement. She feels a thrill of pleasure as she lashes the boy across the back.

Anjar Zimmer: aooffff.

Anjar Zimmer: "No need to whip me ....savage woman," he whisper.

Bysshe Artaud flinches at the crack of the whip and feels a bit sorry for the boy as her eyes move involuntarily to the zigzag of moist red welts on his back.

Alaya Twine pants, her heart beating wildly in her breast. She thrashes him with the whip again, a cruel smile twitching at the corners of her mouth.

Anjar Zimmer cry out in pain.

Alaya Twine strikes him again and again. She watches the red marks appear on his back and the little commas of blood that flicker over the grass.

The animation of Alaya uncoiling her whip was impressive. There was willed venom in the stroke of her arm which was accompanied by a high whistling crack. Needless to say, I was taken aback by Katie's proficiency in and enthusiasm for inflicting pain. Was there a cruel sadistic streak in her? Had she inherited it from me?

IM: Alaya Twine: You want him as a slave? Me and Zo already have a boy so I don't want him.

I had no desire whatsoever to keep Anjar as my slave. I was trying to picture his (or her) owner at his keyboard. How much playful irony, I wondered, was there in his urgent requests for more humiliation. Granted absolute anonymity, as most of these people were, it was somewhat disconcerting to realise how salient was the desire to humiliate, to be humiliated.

I got up and stretched my legs. As I did so I caught an unexpected reflection of myself in the glass of the window. Something about the pale disembodied ghostliness of my own image disconcerted me. I decided to make myself some coffee. The kitchen was way too bright. The abrupt syncopated cadences of Bysshe's world were now constantly pulsating on my retinas. My heart-rate seemed to have increased too – I was making more urgent claims on my blood supply. Through the window I saw the familiar line of terraced houses. The whole road was asleep. One of the morning's first planes set the cutlery jarring on the side of the sink. There was no sense of elapsed time while I accompanied Bysshe on her adventures. It was always shocking and a little shameful to realise how many hours I passed with her. As I waited for the mocca to bubble up its rejuvenating elixir I felt suddenly very alone, but as if on a stage, watched by invisible eyes. I also felt ill again, unsteady on my feet.

I went back to the computer and sent Katie a message:

IM: Bysshe Artaud: Katie…

IM: Bysshe Artaud: You ought to get in touch with your mum. She's very worried about you.

IM: Alaya Twine: WTF. Who are you? You're Charlie, aren't you? You can fuck right off.

Before I had finished composing the big reveal, the full force of the magnitude of which now struck me anew and made every combination of words I came up with wheeze and groan with protests of inadequacy, Bysshe was in orbital freefall, cascading through outer space. The impact of returning to earth left her momentarily in an undignified state of disarray, but she got to her feet with a rather captivating grace. A bleak landscape of lonely roads and grey wasteland slowly came into focus around her. Then some twisted steel girders appeared. Bysshe was standing in front of the ruins of the World Trade Centre. I tried to take her back to the sim where Katie and her tribe lived, but she was forbidden entry. Katie had clearly blocked me. Neither could I send her a message as she had unfriended Bysshe. It suddenly dawned on me that Bysshe had no physical existence in the world.

Katie

1

"I've blocked her from all our sims," says Beth breathlessly as though she has just hurriedly climbed several flights of stairs. Beth is a big girl with tiny breasts. She smells of the distilled essence of several wildflowers. "Of course, her host could create a new avatar and get back in that way. What's the deal?"

Sitting on her bed Katie raises her knees and clasps her ankles. She can feel the presence of her childhood in this posture. "It was someone who knows me in real life. She sent me a message telling me to let my mum know I'm okay."

"Creepy."

"It was. Bloody creepy. Like someone had climbed in through my bedroom window at night."

Before logging off Katie copies all her avatar's interactions with Bysshe Artaud and saves them on a notecard. She will look at it later to confirm her hunch that Bysshe Artaud is an ex-boyfriend's latest way of stalking her. She now picks up her guitar and holds it in her lap without touching the strings.

"I'm logging off for the night as well," says Beth. "I can't face the slave auction without you there to rp with." She gets to her feet and performs some stretching.

"I suppose I ought to let my mother know I'm okay," says Katie.

When Katie thinks of her mother she sees her hunched over

a washbasin scouring away stains. Applying all the vigour of her upper body to the task. Or else she sees her mother's head buried in an opened refrigerator, the stark arctic glare and cornucopia of brightly packaged culinary options. While steam from two shuddering saucepans evaporates on the window, making of the glass a darkening mirror. It's a kitchen where ritual reigns, where every bowl and cup and knife has an allotted consecrated storage place. She knows her mother is essentially well-meaning. But her mother can't help policing her. And like all police her first thought is always for the established order. For Katie, who likes to exaggerate, the established order is penny-pinching, claustrophobic, repressive. Her mother's barricades aren't much different in scope from the establishment's barricades, denying access to the places where decisions are made, laws implemented, payments made and received, injustices and inequalities plotted or covered up.

Katie has read the email from her mother about her father. She knows he arrived completely by chance on their doorstep one day, delivering groceries. She hasn't replied. She needs some time out from her mother. And she is still processing this new knowledge of her father. The first time she saw her father on film she was taken aback that her mother had managed to attract someone so glamorous and sexy. It messed with some founding complacent idea she needs her mother to conform to, as if she had opened her wardrobe to discover the clothes of a stranger hanging there. It has always been a lynchpin of her self-esteem to believe her own spirit is much more pioneering than her mother's. At school there was a period when she studied the older girls, those with a residue of sex on their skin, trying to learn their uninhibited poise, trying to discover how she might make herself the object of envy and desire. It had never occurred to her to study her own mother.

"Do your parents know where you are?" she asks Beth.

"You mustn't tell anyone where you are. Rule number one," says Beth.

Overhead there is the jarring scrape of a table or chair being moved. Then footsteps pacing back and forth.

Sadie now enters the room. Tonight she is wearing a bedraggled blonde wig and a dishevelled lime-green taffeta dress from another era. The heat of the day has drawn a sour mustiness from her second-hand clothes. Like Katie, Sadie has small intricate self-inflicted red abrasions along her arms. They have compared their wounds, the secret script engraved on their flesh. Sadie doesn't use a knife on herself anymore. This house and its community of people, she has told Katie, has cured her of the desire to self-harm. Sadie used to be a street performer. Sometimes she performs her act in the house or garden. She paints her face to look like a doll - heavily rouged cheeks, white face paint and wet coarsely-painted pillar box red lips. She holds a green parasol over her head and does not twitch a muscle for fifteen minutes at a time. Whenever anyone approaches she sticks out her tongue. She has perfected a doll walk too - swinging her arms loosely at her side while performing a quick loose-limbed geisha shuffle as if wound up like a clockwork toy, her feet barely leaving the ground. It reminds Katie of her father's onstage shuffle under the flashing lights. She has watched footage of her father so many times under those lights that the images have almost become like memories of moments she has experienced first-hand. The shifting coloured smoke and shadows in which her father moves oddly reminiscent of the capricious lighting of memory.

Katie shares a room with Sadie and Beth in a sprawling farmhouse, once a monastery, in a remote region of France. It's a room with whitewashed walls of rough-hewn local stone which has undergone little renovation since medieval times. Except there are three rotating cameras with blinking red lights attached to the walls. The cameras track the movements of the girls around the room. Katie still hasn't grown accustomed to them. There are cameras in every room, including the bathrooms, and more cameras in the courtyard and overlooking the wide lawn at the back of the house. She also has to wear a small microphone at all times, like everyone else.

There are about thirty six people living in the farmhouse and its outbuildings. The nearest other habitation is at least a mile distant and the nearest town about ten miles away. Seed, the self-appointed guru of the community, lives in a secluded part of the building with his own high-walled garden. Katie has never set eyes on him. She was surprised when she found out he never leaves his quarters. It was immediately apparent both Beth and Sadie felt uncomfortable speaking his name, as if he was listening, watching. Neither will they tell her in any detail what it is they do here to protest global warming. Seed is never openly discussed by any of the inhabitants. There are whispers though. That he's the head of a large tech company. That he's a retired rock star. That he's from some aristocratic European family. She senses there is something about him no one is telling her. She pictures him with long matted hair and a beard, sitting in front of banks of TV screens. She can't help thinking of him when she undresses for bed at night. She suspects every girl secretly hopes it is her he is watching undress. Sometimes she finds herself wishing she could speak to someone outside the community about the community. To get a better handle on what she feels about living here. She worries that it bears all the hallmarks of a crazed cult and every day has to ask herself if she's being brainwashed. Sometimes she looks closely at all Seed's acolytes to assure herself they don't share any sign of a uniform devotional intensity, that, behind the collective mantra, they display evidence of being engaged in private quests of their own.

One night towards sunrise, unable to sleep, she heard a car pull up nearby. After the last reverberations of the engine died down and the doors were quietly closed, silence rushed back into the ensuing void like water. No matter how hard she strained her ears she could not hear a subsequent sound. It was eerie how careful the occupants of the car were not to make any noise.

2

Katie strips down to her underwear and wades into the creek. Imisa's stunning figure, critically reviewed by Katie, has accentuated her self-consciousness. Especially because Edgar, the boy with the blonde dreadlocks she fancies, is sitting on the bank playing his guitar. The sight of him makes her feel she is holding something warm to her ribs. She has always been attracted to musicians. She perhaps should have known her father would be a musician.

At the creek there are no cameras and they can remove their microphones.

She swims about in the water which is warm on the surface, cold underneath. It feels good to push against an opposing force, to make such precise demands of her body. Then she floats on her back for a while, eyes closed. When she stands up she watches the water wash down over her breasts and taper down into an arrowhead between her legs. She dislikes this view of her body. It highlights the curves at the expense of the lines. She glances over at Edgar. He is still not looking at her. Water-beaded, sun-glistened, she sits down beside Imisa on the opposite bank. Imisa is wearing a lemon-yellow bikini.

"You're always so glamorously dressed," says Katie, holding her face up to the sun.

Imisa smiles, but as if uncertain whether she has been complimented or criticised. Imisa is the girl in the house most often called to the confessional.

"I hate all my clothes," says Katie. "I'd like an entire new wardrobe."

"Seed would probably say that indicates you don't have a lot of love for yourself at the moment."

"Would he? What's he like, Seed?"

"Inspiring. Like the father you wished you had."

"I'm a sucker for father figures."

"Aren't we all?"

"Have you met him? Face to face, I mean."

Katie keeps stealing glances at Edgar.

"Yes. You'll meet him too when you prove yourself."

"What do you mean?"

"Wait and see."

"Everyone's so protective of him, of his mystery. Have you had sex with him?"

Imisa gives her a coy look she can't decipher.

"Don't all cult leaders demand sexual favours of their female initiates? Isn't that, at root, the attraction of becoming a cult leader?"

"If you say so."

"This place is crazy, you know that, right?"

"You're here."

"And that makes me crazy too is what you're saying?"

Imisa lifts her eyebrows a fraction.

"Ciao ragazze."

"Ciao, Furio."

Furio is dripping wet. He stands with his hands on his hips, flushed with testosterone. His rainbow shorts slung low on his hips. Black script tattooed on his tanned chest and on his wrists. Katie resists a mad urge to slide her hand up his thigh and slip it inside his shorts. She sometimes has to resist mad urges. They come to her like Tourette's. One time she had to walk out into the street in the middle of the night because the temptation of stabbing a sleeping boyfriend became so plausible it terrified her.

"Bellissima," he says, kissing his fingers.

"What's bellissima?"

"You are," he says. "Both of you."

Furio possesses a sluggish earthy nature, a sun-kissed laissez-faire attitude. He is clearly a rogue. Katie likes the lack of sincerity in most of what he says. He'll say anything to further his cause with a woman. He has no pretensions to be earnest. His body is his sincerity. Everything else is decoration. He is like a building in which the shape of the stones shows in the walls.

"We were talking about Seed. For Imisa, he is a father figure. What is he to you?"

"That's not what I said," says Imisa.

"For me, he is the ghost in the machine," says Furio, his eyes fixed on the area between Imisa's partially open thighs. "Do you know what he said to me one time? He said the most deeply personal thing about anyone is the smell of their shit."

Katie laughs. "Tell me something else about him."

"You are more beautiful," he says.

"Were you by any chance a gondolier in your former life? I can imagine you serenading women past their prime. You'd be good at it."

"You are not past your prime. Why you think this?"

"That's not what I meant. I fear you will always be lost in translation to me, Furio."

He sits down next to Imisa. "*Comunque*, I was working for Fiat in my former life. *Lavoro importante*. Important job."

"I bet you would be bored stiff at any kind of board meeting," she says. "Unless there was an attractive woman to look at. A woman with a couple of buttons undone and a fidgety mouth."

"Women," he says and smiles. He has a problem saying women in English. He looks for a moment as though he has something unpleasant in his mouth.

"And now you're working for Seed, doing what exactly?"

"We work together. *Come un solo organismo*. As one organism."

They are joined by Hunter and Dodo. Dodo has spiky pink hair, wears a green embroidered petticoat with army boots and flaunts seven rings on her left hand and innumerable bracelets on both wrists. Her legs are tattooed with tiny images of plants and flowers and vines. Hunter is an American prankster who unsettles Katie because of the liberties he takes with his hands. Twice he has lifted her up and carried her over his shoulder. He does this with most of the girls. He enjoys making girls squeal. He now sits beside her and rests his head on her shoulder.

"You know the rules," she says. "Seed doesn't approve of anyone coupling up."

"He doesn't mind us having casual sex though."

"Are you sure he's not some kind of pervert?"

"I dare you to say that into your microphone in the house," says Imisa.

Hunter, Furio and Dodo share a conspiratorial smile.

"Maybe I will," says Katie, knowing she won't. "Why do you all obey him? Isn't a bit mindless?"

"It's his party."

"And like Gatsby he never shows up at his own parties. He just watches. What's that all about? The cameras everywhere. The Big Brother parody. How long does it take before you forget you're under surveillance every minute of every day? I find it exhausting enough being the object of my own obsessive study without others joining in."

"It's just a way of mimicking the world we live in," says Dodo. "But it's not like we're on national TV. It's only Seed watching. And I doubt if he does watch. He's got more important stuff to think about. Probably it's just a bit of fun. Or some kind of social experiment he's conducting. I never think about the cameras."

"Haven't you always imagined someone is watching you, whatever you do?" says Imisa. "Experience for me doesn't take root unless there's a witness. Isn't that why everyone posts photos of themselves on social media? On film, the most banal everyday moments become history, and we all know how much power history has."

"I bet that's a Seed quote," says Dodo.

"He might have said something similar to me once upon a time."

"I've heard on the grapevine we're sharing a room at the next switch," says Hunter, tickling her naval. Katie shoves him off.

"Did Beth tell you we all change rooms every so often? It keeps us on our toes."

"She told me. And that Seed decides the rosters."

"As long as I don't get the scorpion room."

"What's that?"

"A downstairs room where scorpions like to hang out," says Dodo.

"*Scorpioni. Scorpioni e serpenti*," says Furio, close to Imisa's ear. He nuzzles his face in her neck. Allows the back of his hand to brush a line across her naval.

"What about environmentalist action?" says Katie. "Isn't that supposed to be the point of the place? I'm not seeing much of that. I'm not seeing *any* of that. Am I going to have to camp out high in the branches of a tree at some point?"

"Maybe. I've done that. It's a beautiful experience. Mind altering," says Dodo. "Trees can talk. I bet you didn't know that. They can communicate with the world around them. And they write their own history. Something we should all be able to do."

Katie smiles with what she hopes is empathy. She doesn't want to cast doubt on the ardent thrust of Dodo's narrative. She respects all big-hearted communions with life. "It's just that I was hoping we would be making a more significant contribution to the fight against global warming," she says.

"If you only knew."

"Tell me."

"Hunter," says Imisa in a warning tone.

"We can trust Katie."

"Can we trust you, Katie?"

"Let's just say there was a large sawmill that mysteriously burnt to the ground last month."

"That's three days in the punishment cell for you, Hunter."

"What's the punishment cell?"

"Just a joke."

"Global warming is the most pressing issue of our age and yet its causes, often the insatiable greed of corporations, are hardly ever a feature of mainstream news," says Imisa. "A politician gets caught screwing his secretary and it's a headline story; swathes of life-supporting forest are razed to the ground and no news-caster even mentions it. We're doing what we can to get global warming onto the mainstream news."

Furio has rolled a joint. He takes several deep draughts and then hands it to Imisa.

Over on the opposite bank Edgar is now singing to himself while playing the guitar. The lyrics of his song drift across the glittering water.

I want to hold the hand inside you
I want to take the breath that's true
I look to you and see nothing
I look to you and see the truth.

3

Sometimes Katie is on kitchen duty; sometimes cleaning; sometimes laundry. She sings to herself while she works. She wishes she had a better singing voice. She tells Beth it is fascinating to discover what kind of underwear each individual wears. Like a litmus test of how much sexual vanity they harbour, even of how they experience their sexuality. She enjoyed holding Edgar's unclean shorts in her hands. She likes sometimes to imagine herself as a wife. Laughingly, she caressed her face with them in front of Beth. "Hopefully he'll do that with my knickers when he's on laundry duty," she said.

There are tech tutorials, occasional film studies and lectures, work out sessions. Later, at three in the morning, there is to be a war paint ceremony. Katie, as a new member of the family, will be anointed in her colours and symbols. And then a sapling will be planted in her honour. Seed has chosen a magnolia for her. She will be expected to commune with the tree for at least half an hour every day.

"No doubt there will be more drama tonight with Furio. The two of us are definitely enacting some kind of karmic realignment of traumatic residues," says Beth in a tone of matter-of-fact finality as if reading out a maxim in a Christmas cracker. "He touched my shoulder earlier and I melted down the front of my dress. I dreamt about him last night. I was climbing a tree and he was sitting beneath watching me. Then I realised I wasn't wearing any knickers underneath my skirt. That's exactly how he makes me feel. That I'm not wearing any knickers. Do you know what I mean?"

"Furio is having sex with Imisa. I know because I'm jealous. Not of her. Of him," says Katie.

Beth turns bright red, like a stop sign. Katie can feel the rush of fierce heat in her body. Sadie performs a nervous giggle.

"Sorry. I shouldn't have told you."

"She knows I like him. She always has to piss over my territory. Oh, I love Imisa; of course I love her to bits, but do you know what really hacked me off? I went into her room and saw the big portrait of the Dalai Lama over her bed. I've been searching for ages for a portrait of the Dalai Lama and she knew it. I ended up feeling that it's because she's all pure and angelic and thin that the Dalai Lama manifested a picture of himself for her and not for me."

"Should I be nervous about this ceremony tonight?"

"It's fun," says Sadie. She sits cross legged in the midst of a miscellany of crumpled ball gowns, wigs, lace, linen and satin lingerie whose original owners are probably long since dead. Today she is wearing a flouncy tattered red dress. Under the black wig of curls, she has a shaved head. Sadie is much more beautiful when she is not wearing one of her bedraggled wigs. When Katie told her this, she shook her head back and forth in giggling denial.

Beth has told her that Sadie's mother's older sister was a member of Charles Manson's family. There is news footage of her protesting outside the courthouse when he and the girls were on trial for the murders. A young girl in a skimpy summer dress with a radiant light in her eyes. Katie now watches Sadie do her doll scuttle across the room.

"You walk like my father did on stage."

Katie brings up the YouTube video of him and his band performing 'Shadow and Sun' at the Drury Lane Theatre.

"Fuck, he's gorgeous," says Beth.

"I've never met him. Only found out he's my father a couple of years ago."

"He does shuffle around like you, Sadie. Look, it's like his feet never leave the ground. Except you're a doll and he's like some kind of android."

Sadie giggles and shakes her head back and forth.

Later, Katie is called to the confessional for the first time. The disembodied male voice that suddenly resonates through the high echoing room startles her. She looks across at Beth in alarm. "Do you think I've done something wrong?"

"I never get called anymore," says Beth quietly with a churlish note, as if to herself. "No, I don't think you've done anything wrong. It's about time you were called to the confessional. Think yourself lucky. Probably Seed wants to get to know you."

Katie goes out into the courtyard, looks up briefly at the moon, climbs some outside steps up to an arched gallery with an iron grill built into the thick wall and sunken windows. A boy and a girl are sitting on a wicker sofa sharing a laptop. They both say hi. She walks through a kind of conservatory with views of both the courtyard and garden succumbing to darkness. She is now close to Seed's part of the house. His rooms are somewhere around the next corner. The cold iron bracelet of the confessional door startles her into realising how hot her body is. Inside is a small dark vaulted room with no window. There's a smell of damp plaster and stone and a nimbus of trapped dust. The only light is provided by a montage of filmed images streaming over the whitewashed walls: a prowling lioness in a cage, crashing surf, running deer, seabirds gummed in oil, an old Hindu man at prayer, a forest fire, a river choked with plastic, a polar bear on a floe of ice, a simulation of the moment a meteor hit Earth, two lovers in Venice, a swan feeding her cygnets, the Northern Lights, a speeded up film of the blossoming and decay of a red rose, God and Adam on the Sistine Ceiling, Holocaust corpses, a North American Indian dancing in full regalia. Katie sits down on the varnished wooden bench. Suddenly a deep male voice with a whispery echo speaks to her.

"Any impure thoughts to confess, Katie?"

Katie looks up at the camera. Her body heats up with some unidentifiable rush of guilt.

"I'm just joking, Katie. This isn't a Catholic confessional and I'm certainly no priest."

She understands this is Seed talking to her. She can't remember ever being so intimidated in her life. She imagines telling a friend, it was like talking to a deity.

"Night is coming down. Time of desire. Time of recrimination." His voice is measured and slow and hypnotic, like drifting snow. "Anything on your mind, Katie?"

She thinks about telling him she is losing track of all the rhythms of her normal life, not necessarily a bad thing.

"I hope you feel you've begun mapping out some new coordinates in your mind," he says.

"Are you a mind reader?" she says and laughs.

"I can be, if that's what you want from me."

"What I sometimes feel I want is simply to feel myself naked, aroused and slightly out of my depth," she says, because her first instinct with new people is always to show off, to publicise the creative footwork of her mind. She smiles up at the camera. Then she looks down at the black line of her knickers above the waistband of her red skirt.

"You've arrived here with me because you've refused the future that was on offer to you. You believe you're worthy of a better future. And you are worthy of a better future. But first you'll need to take off your mask."

"What mask?"

"Your performing mask. You spend too much of your energy caricaturing yourself and those around you for comedy. You want to create theatre of your life. And unless you feel you have the starring role you are wretched. Isn't that why you make incisions in your flesh? A mask can be expedient when it's a mask you know you're wearing and can take off at will, but masks which are worn habitually cannot be removed without tearing off some of your real face."

"I'm not sure that's true," she says, disorganised by the force of this surprise attack on her equanimity.

"You're too centred in your vanity, Katie. Your intelligence, because you have so little real confidence in yourself, is essentially sentimental. Might it not be said that you've still not outgrown the pleasure principle of a child? That you're a prisoner of your own narcissism?"

She feels her ears and cheeks catch fire. It's another of those moments when she hates her body. Her body is always giving away her secrets. She knows she sometimes disappears into the nervous insincerity of her performances. But what right, even with his kind and interested tone of voice, has he got pointing this out? Her immediate instinct is to tell him to fuck off.

"I once had a girlfriend who said my insights probed over her nakedness like hands inside rubber gloves. That I always had to seek out any corrupt and slovenly element in her feeling and hold it up to the light. But my truth is that, essentially, we're like flowers - we have an evolutionary imperative, an informed sense of what we have it in ourselves to become, which originates in the dark and slowly creates the conditions that enable us to fulfil our nature. What must be does not come by chance. There's a dance inside you, Katie. An entire beautiful choreography which belongs to you and no one else. And it has organic roots. Do not damage those roots."

Katie is at a loss for words. His voice slides and oozes all over her like liquid mud. It's as if he wants to force her back into a dark place within where she can no longer see herself.

"I discovered earlier you're the daughter of Nick Swallow. Truth be told, I had never heard of him. But I once played bass guitar in a band and I checked him out. Let me tell you, your father made the bass a thing of beauty."

"Thank you," she says, surly, still bristling with antagonism. "Except I've never met him."

"I'm sorry to hear that. We all need a father. If only for the illuminating opposition he unwittingly or unwillingly provides. That said, it's the fathers of the world who are responsible for destroying our planet for our children and our children's children. Because they haven't learned the true values, the core priorities of fatherhood. In most indigenous tribes, scope is allowed for personal gain, but every father's foremost thought is for the responsible husbandry of communal resources."

Any mention of fathers always used to lead Katie to the tidal flats of a cold stony windswept beach in her mind. As if it was there her own father had arranged to meet her. But he never appeared, and never was she able to pick up his scent, follow him inland, know what he thought, listen to what he said, react to what he felt. The effort always summoned up an echoing void within her which made her mind race in the dark. Her mind still races in the dark. Like a spinning spool from which tape is riotously escaping. She has tried using drugs and alcohol and sex to stop her mind from racing. It's why she craves friends who will do more than they are asked. It's why she is always anxious for something new to happen. Why there are times when she seeks a man for whom she is nothing less than the entire cosmos. A man who will take her to the centre of his being and make a home there for her.

"I'm making you part of the fieldwork team next week. You'll have to learn the discipline of stalking. Now go and enjoy the war paint ceremony. And thank you for talking with me, Katie."

4

Katie is wearing a short denim skirt and a crop top which reveals her tanned midriff and the glinting stud of silver in her belly button. Her bitten-down fingernails have chipped ice-blue paint on them. She greets Furio, the object of Beth's obsession. The habitual pleased expression on his face, as if he is recalling a night his fingers had gone probing inside some girl's knicker elastic. A large pair of headphones are clamped around his neck. He dresses as boys do in fashion magazines. There is always a blob of spittle dancing around on his tongue when he speaks. "Ciao," he says, hands deep in his fake paratrooper trouser pockets. She looks around for Edgar. *I want to hold the hand inside you/ I want to take the breath that's true.* The recollection of his song slides a discharge of warm feeling down underneath her clothes.

Beacons of fire are arranged in a wide circle on the lawn. A breeze intermittently scatters showers of sparks up into the air. The flames throw huge jittery shadows over the grass. The stars are bright overhead. A large bare-chested man, who Beth whispers to her is security, stands in front of a large handmade drum. Another bare-chested man holds a handmade flute. They both look fierce and frightening in the uncertain light of the fires. Then a teenage girl appears. She wears a single upright feather in her braided hair. There are four painted handprints, two green and two red, on the beaded and tasselled dress she wears. Her necklace is made of painted animal teeth. She looks like an elegant creature from another world.

"That's Wachiwi. We think she's Seed's daughter," whispers

Sadie who is out of costume tonight. She is wearing black slacks and army boots and no wig hides her shaved head. She speaks in her natural voice. It is deeper, more sensual. Not the contrived high giggly sing-song voice she uses when dressed as a doll. "Isn't she beautiful? She's half Lakota."

"What's that?"

"Native American. The Sioux. You know, Crazy Horse and Sitting Bull. The tribe that made Custer eat dirt."

The man with the flute produces a series of shrill echoing notes. A breeze blows a wave of scented smoke over Katie. She feels it on her neck, in her hair. Shadows swell and gather around her. They seem alive, pulsating and breathing, rhythmic and graceful, like a circle of ghost dancers. The large man begins pounding his drum and chanting. Wachimi begins to dance. She has tiny bells tied around her ankles. Painted ribbons of cloth flutter from her waist. She shifts her weight gracefully from one foot to the other and moves forwards and backwards in elegant little jumps. Lightly pawing the ground with her feet as if the earth is a responding living thing, as if the earth is a lover. Every so often she turns a circle and goes back on her tracks in strange birdlike hops. Her head rocking from side to side. The drum pounds. Becomes the rhythm of Katie's heartbeat as she watches. When Wachimi stretches out her arms the fringed wide sleeves of her dress look like wings. She bobs delicately up and down, tassels swaying. Like a bird leaving a message on the ground. Like a bird that at any moment might take flight. Every movement is measured. She follows a map already plotted. There is no improvisation. It makes Katie realise how little of her own life is measured. She has been on and off medication for two years. The thrust of her mind rarely linear and progressive, and the tracks over which it travels rarely clamped down with steadfast and secure engineering. Every comforting thought slides from one side of her mind to the other without catching a cog. Or else she feels recklessly elated as if cycling downhill without hands, without breaks. Most often she feels like she is standing on the threshold of her life, denied entry, like a ghost bound by some psychic law to haunt ad infinitum the same small enclosure of space. She once told her psychotherapist: "Sometimes I think the more one thinks the less ground one has to stand on."

Wachimi looks solemn and beautiful in the circle of phosphorescence made by the lights of the fire. She is like the mystery of gravity made more apparent. Katie is mesmerised by how secret she makes herself as she dances, as if she is alone in her own dreamscape, as if she is bringing forth a reality ordinarily only achieved in dreams.

And the flames in the darkness make Katie feel more feral and unknown to herself.

5

When Katie is told she has to strip naked to be painted she refuses.

"We all did it," says Dodo. "You have to be in your natural state for this ceremony."

"You have to demonstrate your trust in us," says Imisa.

"And you've got a great body."

"Shut up, Hunter."

She contemplates storming off set. She wants to tell them they are all crazy. For a moment she is her mother. Policing the situation at hand. She begins to talk hurriedly, mocking and belittling, making sweeping hand gestures. A way she has of trying to expel the demons in her mind. She grips a fistful of her top and plucks it from her chest. She tugs at the hair at the back of her head. She can't subdue the desire for violence in her hands. She is deaf to all entreaties from outside her own head.

Initially, the dance of Wachimi left her feeling good about herself. But then it began to make her feel inadequate. As she was compelled to admit she herself was incapable of ever carrying herself with such grace, of shining such a beatific light on the world around her. And one of her dark destructive moods took hold of her. Jealousy, when another girl steals the limelight, can paint her soul black. She hates this insecure trait in her with its snapping iron teeth, like a trap primed in the underbrush of her being. When a boyfriend once told her a friend of hers had a better body than she did she barely slept for two nights afterwards. Eaten up with hatred for this man, for the entire male sex. Her mother told her, *Men encourage women to be competitive to acquire power over them.* But knowing the cypher of a trick doesn't necessarily defuse its charge. Now she feels her self-esteem doesn't possess the resilience or resources to strip naked in front of a group of strangers and hidden cameras. There's a new boy who is to be painted too. He has stripped naked with barely a qualm. But males aren't trained to proof-read their naked bodies the way females are. Rationally, she knows there's nothing ugly about her body. But her hips are too wide and her breasts too small and she is capable of magnifying these two misgivings into disfigurements as if her entire body is covered in open ugly festering sores.

"It was the most difficult thing I've ever had to do," says Beth. "It's like my biggest hang-up. Being naked in front of people. But I felt so much better about myself afterwards. Like I was liberated of ego."

"Who's Ego? Ex-boyfriend?" wisecracks Hunter.

"Shut up, Hunter."

"But seriously, come on, Katie. You can do it."

Then Seed's voice, like an aural apparition, resonates out of a hidden loudspeaker into the night. "Love can make us bold. Fear can make us mean. Fear can push us towards hatred. Sometimes your tasks will require the hatred that fear helps generate. Sometimes you will have to be viciously hateful. But always on a basis of love. The love we feel for the encompassing wonder of the natural world which supports us and makes every breath we take possible."

Everyone has been startled into attention. Everyone avoids eye contact with anyone else. Katie feels resolve leak out of her in the semireality of what's taking place, as if it's suddenly irrelevant whether or not she agrees to remove her clothes.

"However, I don't want anyone forced to do anything they don't want to do. Tonight Katie will be allowed to wear her underwear."

Seed's concession, which should irritate her with its puppet master effrontery, instead makes her feel better, partly because he has singled her out and partly because she senses it arouses jealousy in some of the other girls. She undresses in the light of the fires. A breeze arrives and lifts some burning leaves into the air. She can see the flitting liquid green lights of fireflies among the myrtle leaves, over where she has planted her magnolia sapling. She can feel the pulse of the earth through her bare feet on the grass.

Opposite her, the new boy Rodrigo is being painted by three girls, including Imisa who is wearing hot pants. They use their hands to apply the pigment. They paint black and red stripes across his eyes and a series of blue dots under his left eye. When Imisa kneels down to paint his naval, his penis quivers and rises. His face turns bright red. Thank heavens I don't have that problem, Katie thinks. Three boys are smearing paint over her. Furio is the best looking of the three. Then there's Hunter and Raine. Raine's features and the pigmentation of his skin are a hybrid of just about every racial physiognomy known to man. Raine refuses to talk about the past. He says memories can't be digitised and as such are obsolete in the modern world. Katie tries to separate the hands of the males touching her, connect them to the personality of their owners. Furio, she senses, is trying his best to turn her on. This is just another challenge for his sexual vanity. His fingers are pressing paint to the insides of her thighs. Hunter's hands are clumsy and over-eager, like everything else about him. Raine's touch is fussily methodical, like the knot in the tie of a newsreader. She has been told Seed chose the designs. The boys each have a computer printout which they intermittently study.

When the ceremony is over Beth takes her into the house to see herself in a mirror. Her face is painted black and blue with a red stripe running down her nose and over her mouth to her chin. There are red splashes under her eyes. A rudimentary green and gold snake coiled around the length of her leg. Small black circles printed all over her torso. She doesn't recognise herself in the mirror. She is unsettled by her new appearance, as if this girl facing her is capable of deeds undreamed of by her familiar self.

"How do you feel?"

"I don't know. Frisky. Like I want to go into the woods and have wild sex with one of the boys."

Beth laughs. "In an ideal world nobody would ever have sex which wasn't a liberating communion with the dark gods. But we all need to make mistakes."

"You do say the most extraordinary things."

"Thanks. Any particular boy taken your fancy?"

In the mirror Katie catches sight of the shifting kaleidoscope of rainbow lights in the crystal hanging above Beth's bed. "Edgar would be my first choice, but I'm not feeling too fussy tonight. Who's that man who never talks to anyone. With the piercing blue eyes and beard."

"Zivko. You don't like him, do you?"

"No gravitational pull there whatsoever. Just the opposite. He gives me the creeps. He's the only person here I'm not sure I like."

"He's okay. Just does his own thing. He's been here longer than anyone. Probably arrived with Seed. There's a lot of Pluto in him."

"What does that mean?"

"Pluto is the great humbler. Without Pluto our hubris would know no bounds."

"If you ask me he looks like he could kill another human being without too many qualms."

She has forgotten Seed might be listening and instantly regrets what she says. She doesn't want it reaching Zivko that she doesn't like him. The thought of making an enemy of him frightens her.

6

Katie is on kitchen duty the following morning, preparing and serving breakfast. She stands stirring the large battered saucepan of porridge. Her skin is slippery with sweat.

"Add the honey and cinnamon after you take it off the flame," says Beth who is soaking lentils for tonight's supper.

Everyone is seated at the enormous wooden refectory table. There is a fresco on one of the walls depicting various mammals, reptiles, birds and insects. Every species depicted, she has been told, is on the verge of extinction. Every month a new creature has to be added. The painting is a lamentation over worlds either vanishing or lost completely. Somewhere beneath the kitchen is a mysterious underground bunker where, she has been told, the tech guys work. She still doesn't know if this was a joke. There's also a large pantry which is stockpiled with dried food and household necessities. "In case there's a pandemic," she has been told. "Seed believes there will be a pandemic sooner rather than later."

Sadie is performing her statuesque doll routine. Standing frozen in a limp pose on her green trunk in her flouncy red dress by the large fireplace. Because she's so good at making believe she has no interiority, no female plumbing, it doesn't surprise Katie that she acted as a magnet to unloved, unhinged men with misogynist fetishes out on the streets of Paris, Prague and Budapest. Sadie has told her about some of them. Men who really believed she was a doll. Men who got angry when she answered back.

Zivko is reading a copy of *Helter Skelter* when Katie brings one of the vats of porridge to the table. She tries to imagine him looking at himself in a mirror. He doesn't appear to care what he looks like. She earlier spent some time looking at her reflection after showering off her war paint. She studied herself frontally and then in profile. She raised her chin and sucked in her cheeks. Pouting, she gathered her long hair up in a knot and then let it fall back down around her face. The features from which she sought eloquence began to recede behind a haze of film until her face no longer quite seemed to belong to her. Always this happened when she deemed herself attractive in glass. Her beauty disappeared. As a child she had often leant against the trunk of the garden's cherry tree, ran her hand over the bark, tracing the end of one cycle and the beginning of another. She would clasp the trunk and begin trying to shake it. Why would not the tree shake its blossom over her? This is how she feels whenever face to face with her beauty in the mirror - it will never shake its blossom over her.

Hunter now gathers her by the waist and pulls her down into his lap.

"This is what I want for *my* breakfast," he says. She feels the greedy warmth of his body seep down into her loins. She looks down at his hands on the waistband of her skirt. He has little tufts of black hair on his knuckles and his finger joints are stubbly. They are unmusical hands. They are not hands she can imagine playing a guitar. It's an unwritten law of hers never to sleep with any man whose hands wouldn't suit a guitar. She looks over at Edgar who is wearing a torn black t-shirt and sunglasses.

"I liked your song yesterday," she says.

Edgar nods, non-committal, cool, as if feeling himself under too much scrutiny to reveal any more of himself. He is good at making himself difficult to read. She feels Hunter flinch. She hadn't meant to hurt him, but now she has she finds she wants to hurt him some more. She turns to him and sings the line from Edgar's song: "When I look at you I see nothing."

Imisa smiles over at her. The top she is wearing has slipped off one shoulder disclosing the curve of her breast inside a black bra of gossamer and lace. Given the choice, Katie would have sex with Imisa rather than with Hunter. She has tapering sensitive fingers which make anything they touch appear more valuable.

When she has finished her duties she walks out into the courtyard and holds her face up to the rising sun. A bough of young leaves is turned into a staff of flickering green drops of light. Two male peacocks shuffle about over the paving stones. The windows of Seed's apartment are visible from the courtyard, but always covered by fastened blue shutters. Everything she sees - the ripening grapes on the vines, wisteria arching over old walls, a rusted bucket in which rainwater has collected - is as if drawn through a veil into a timeless realm.

Furio joins her outside. But he is wearing his headphones and begins dancing as if she isn't there. It irritates her how conclusively he erases her presence. She watches him throw back his shoulders and make imperious flat-palmed signals with his outstretched hands as if he is putting to rest the misgivings of an entire populace stationed somewhere beyond his swaying body. Then she forgives him as she realises it is probably an optimistic sign for the future of the planet that young white boys now aspire at times to be black. As if, finally, there is no border, no language problem, between black and white. For her stepfather there definitely had been a border and a language problem. Few things in her life have disgusted her more than the covert racism in so much of what her stepfather, self-importantly, had to say for himself.

She walks over to the outside tap, turns it on, cups her hands and throws the icy water up into her face. She is imagining Seed is watching her.

Later she is reading on her bed when she hears a car crunch gravel outside. She walks over to the window. Beth joins her. Zivko is driving. She watches Edgar, Dodo, Imisa and Raine, all wearing backpacks, climb into the dirty white car. And then they drive off. Katie feels cheated. She had intended taking her guitar to the creek in the hope Edgar would be there.

"Where are they going?"

"Not for us to know," says Beth.

They still aren't back at supper time.

Sadie is called to the confessional. Katie discovers she is disappointed when no call arrives summoning her there.

The next day, at breakfast, Dodo has cuts on her hands and a bruise under her left eye and Imisa limps on a sprained ankle.

7

Katie is summoned to the confessional two days later. She makes a pact with herself: don't try to impress him tonight. Again she sits looking at a quickfire montage of images: the uncoiling of a cobra, a waterfall at sunset, a lone oriental fisherman standing in his vessel, a fluctuating matrix of phosphorescent digits, a festival crowd at night, a tornado, a legion of bats entering a cave, a strip of the turquoise sea glittering with renewed verve after chronicling the passage of a seabird's shadow, an African woman leading naked children through a dust storm, the Forum and its oracle of gleaming stones, a lion mounting a lioness, a naked blonde woman performing a pantomime of aroused female sexuality. Except this time, inserted into the flow of spliced footage, is a clip of her father, heavily made-up, black and blue hair slicked back, performing his shuffle and android smirk under spotlights, and including a close up of his fingers slapping at the strings of his bass guitar. Katie sees again he has astonishingly beautiful hands. She has always liked her own hands. The bass has a rich and resonant stress of phrasing and the notes slide into each other with a kind of gorgeous muddy fluidity, burrowing into her loins, becoming part of the flow of her blood. She catches an insight from her father's filmed face. She senses he is an indoors person; she herself is usually tense or bored indoors; she feels much less suffocated outdoors. In this sense they are directly opposed.

"Hello Katie. How are you?"

"You put up a clip of my dad." It sends an electrical trill through her to call him her dad. As if for a moment she is new to herself. She only ever referred to him as him when discussing him with her mother.

"Yes. 'Scorched Earth' - great song."

"I like 'The Touch of Ghosts' better," she says. She feels a need to disagree with him. To push him away. To stop him insinuating himself into her thoughts.

"Let me see the incisions you cut into your arms, Katie."

She wraps herself up in her arms. Makes fists of her hands. "Are you deliberately setting out to humiliate me?"

"Let me see, Katie. And describe to me your state of mind when you wielded the knife."

She resists for a while but finally rolls up the sleeve of her blouse and holds out her wrist to the camera. "Obviously it was an expression of the disgust I felt at myself. Like getting drunk and calling up men in the middle of the night. Forcing them to reject me, forcing them to hold me in contempt."

"Not disgust with the world you were forced to live in, disgust with always having to submit to authority figures who possess for you no authority?"

"Same thing, isn't it? Disgust, when it's pouring out, slops over everything."

"Once you build up the momentum you can do anything you set your mind upon. It isn't hard to build up momentum. You just have to turn your mind into a lens and find the focus. Imagine yourself poised on a high diving board, Katie. You've forged a moment where there are only two choices. To do it or not to do it. There you stand. The moment before the electrifying shock of immersion. On the edge of that high precipice there is an end and there is a beginning. The leap into emptiness is the quest for wisdom. It is an act of surrender. It is the erasing of personal history. The transfiguring of self into simplicity. The entering, body and soul, into a new element. The submersion. The immersion. The brand new moment."

Every expression he manages to bring up onto her face has tension in it.

"I'm going to tell you a story. You must never repeat this to anyone else. My father owned a company which did a lot of damage to the planet. My older brother was set to further our father's legacy. When my brother was nineteen he went on a safari to Africa. He wanted to shoot a lion. That was the horizon of his aspiration. The oasis in his desert. He wanted to impress our father and all his executive cronies. One night my brother and the ranger pitched a tent in the national park. The ranger left the tent unzipped. He left his rifle in the jeep. In the middle of the night a pride of lions discovered the tent. A lion will never kill anything it can't see. And as a rule it doesn't much care for the taste of human flesh. But one of the lionesses in this pride was badly injured and she was starving. When she put her head inside the unzipped tent there was a choice. My brother or the ranger. I'm guessing my brother was closer. Or perhaps he smelled better. She dragged my brother out of the tent. The other lions watched. My brother was screaming. The best plan of action the ranger could come up with was to set fire to his shirt and wave it about. As if the flames might frighten the lions away. They didn't. The lioness didn't drag my screaming brother very far before she began eating him. I've tried to imagine myself inside my brother at that moment so many times in my life. But we can never imagine what it's like to be inside someone else, even someone who shares our own blood. We are all entirely unique, Katie. No one can enter another's mind. The lioness tore off steaks of my brother in the light of a burning shirt. I suppose there must be a few more gruesome ways to die but it requires imagination to picture them. As a result of my brother's death I inherited everything when my father died. And I was able to redirect all his resources. Not immediately, because I had some lessons to learn first. That's all I have to say today, Katie. Thank you for listening."

8

Katie is sitting on a cushion in the back of the van driven by Zivko. She is repeatedly jolted and thrown off-balance. She has not been allowed to bring a single possession with her except the clothes she wears. Not even a bottle of water; not even a cigarette. Earlier, she spoke to her magnolia tree. She told it about the appearance of her father at her mother's home. She asked if she ought to leave this place and return home. Then she told the tree how much she liked Edgar. That it was probably him, more than anything, that kept her here.

Rodrigo is sitting opposite, a thicker outline of shadow in the darkness with ghostly features picked out by the thin drifting light of occasional streetlamps. She senses his hands are clenched into fists, as if holding onto something precious he is fearful of losing. He is wearing a belligerent deodorant.

"Do you understand the point of this?" she asks him.

He doesn't reply. A couple of times in the house she has tried without success to engage this unattractive young man who rarely ever says anything, who just smiles inanely back at you when you talk to him. He has a habit of sucking at his lips which makes him look like he is swirling medicine about in his mouth. His silence now has a critical quality, as if he doesn't find her worthy of his attention.

"As I understand it, we have to stalk each other in the darkness. Experience ourselves as both hunter and hunted. But what's the point? How is that going to save the planet?"

Silence.

"What kind of stuff does Seed say to you when you go to the confessional? Does he lecture you? Does he try to make you feel misguided and small?"

The silence has become more uncomfortable. It begins to irritate her that he is creating this unsettling current on which her inner demons are feeding.

"Must have been embarrassing when you got a hard-on during the war paint ceremony," she says, inclined now to make him absorb some of her discomfort.

He is still silent, but she can feel the heat of his embarrassment as if it is conveyed to her along an invisible wire.

She tries to remember if she has ever heard him speak. There's something pathological about his determination not to speak. As if dammed up behind his silence are violent floodwaters. She is relieved when the van stops and Hunter opens the doors.

"This is your point of departure, Rod. Katie, you wait here."

Rodrigo climbs out of the van without looking at her. Katie sits alone in the stationary vehicle. She soon becomes irritated, weary of her thoughts, unable to make allowances for herself. Then she hears footsteps and the van starts up again. Bumps along what feels like a dirt road. Five minutes later Hunter opens the rear doors. As she's about to jump out he picks her up and carries her over his shoulder. His nervous hands seem always at a loose end unless they have something to hold, like those of someone on ice groping for something to help restore a sense of balance. She looks around. The tall shadowed trees on either side look as ancient and hallowed as the moon and stars. She catches Zivko's eye through the misted glass of the windscreen. She feels suddenly thankful for the presence of Hunter who she can at least trust not to do her any harm. The headlights of the van spray otherworldly sheen over the wooded surroundings. The leaves and bark of nearby trees as if magnified in bewitching detail. Hunter carries her towards a darker place among the trees.

"You know what's expected of you? You've got to stalk Rodrigo. Or else make it home without him finding you. Winner takes all."

"I don't want to do this," she says.

"Don't worry. You'll be back at the house in an hour."

"What's the point?"

"Don't you ever listen to what people say to you?"

"Not when I'm bored, no."

"This is an exercise to sharpen your senses. Become more alone with yourself. Make an ally of the darkness and the natural world. Experience yourself as both predator and prey. Deploying fear as a weapon. Why not think of it as a game of hide and seek? You enjoyed that as a kid, I take it."

"I can't remember ever playing it."

It is true though that she feels more closely connected to her childhood, about to respond to a dare.

"Tell me something, Katie," he says, in a tone of deep serious-ness, as if he is about to change the tenor of their relationship forever. "What's your favourite sex position?" His laughter, spi-ralling out into the solidifying darkness, seems to alert hidden eyes to their presence. "Actually, you'll have to tell me at a later date because this is where I leave you." He makes a lunge at her, kisses her lightly on the lips. She immediately wipes her mouth with the back of her hand.

The darkness seems to become more sentient, more press-ing as she listens to him walk away, crunching bracken beneath his boots. The trees close in on her. Like the forests of her own thoughts when she is feeling lonely and lost. All around her she senses the presence of concealed worlds and creatures in hiding. She feels an ominous shift in her mind's equilibrium. Suddenly she knows the fearful loneliness that she has always associated with the absence of a father in her life. As a girl she often imag-ined her unknown father was watching her. He was her most prized secret. Only she could feel his presence. Sometimes she showed off for his benefit. Other times she collected gifts for him. In her imagination her unknown father sought to embolden her in her desires. He it was, she imagined, who enticed her to dive off a rock into the sea; who escorted her onto the frozen pond in her ice skates. During the day her imaginary father tended to be easier to win over - he dwelled in the sunlight, in the scent of flowers, in moments of communion and self-containment; at night, however, it was his habit to become less protective, more critical and she felt his presence in shadows and untraceable noises.

Katie listens to the van drive off. The brooding spacious night is suddenly an unstruck sound, anticipated on every nerve of her body. It's as if new knowledge is about to enter her, perform its alchemy in her blood. A breeze stirs into prominence the scent with which she has anointed her body. For a moment she smells herself as she would smell to others - off-hand, imperious, seductive. The sham of it almost makes her smile to herself. At every noise it's as if a swarm of bats take flight inside her mind, flit around in panicked circles. She remains statuesque, like Sadie, barely able to make out any detail in the billowing of thicker darkness ahead. An invasive intimacy pulses all around her. It's like the cloying attention of an insistent suitor. When she begins walking the stress of her footsteps reverberates up into her groin, making her feel vulnerably naked to herself. The darkness forces her to adjust her habitual stride. She doesn't recognise her body in its movements. There is a rustling in the undergrowth to her right. Twigs snap beneath her feet. Every noise she makes summons closer an enemy in her imagination. Every step edges her closer to the imagined murder scene.

The spiced smell of ferns and bracken and resin from the bark of the trees enters deep into her lungs. She tastes primal fear in her mouth. A deeper silence than any she has known clings to the undersides of leaves. At the same time there is a booming in her ears as of ocean waves enacting their ritual of onslaught and relapse. She remembers Rodrigo. That he has been tasked with stalking her. She makes the decision to escape the intimate bristling press and thrust of the giant trees, to find her way back to the road and follow it back to the house.

More than once panic overcomes her as she blunders into

impassable thorned barriers. She hyperventilates. It is as if there is a perilous current running through the night against which she is not insulated. The weight of her fear drains strength from her legs and arms. She is in constant intimate dialogue with her body. Everything she can't see she can feel as a presence on her skin and in her blood. She is exhausted and irritable when she finally stumbles upon an unlit road, unsure if it is the same road they earlier drove along.

She looks up at the dwarfing presence of the night sky. The stars tonight have no comfort to offer her. As if their secretive map of lights is a gift to someone else and she is no more than an insignificant bystander.

She has been walking for about an hour when the treeline begins to press up closer to her. Further down the road she hears a low hissing noise. It comes from amongst the trees. Then, when she stops, the hissing ceases. When she moves again the hissing returns on the same note. She stops and the hissing ceases again. She is breathing hard, as if she has been running at full speed. She thinks she will never be able to move again because she cannot bear to hear that noise again. All her muscles are tightly clenched. Her feet feel distant from her body. Her hands are equally difficult to locate. She has the sensation she is being watched. Then she knows it as a certainty. Something in the darkness is studying her. She takes a tentative step forward. A shadow figure slides into view, detaching itself from heavier blackness. The ground beneath her feet tilts. A scream rises in her throat. The shadowed figure shines a torch at her and then up at the horned animal mask it wears. The scream emerges on a piercing raucous animal note. And then she begins running in the opposite direction. It is all she can do to retain her shape, to remain upright.

9

Katie awakes in an unfamiliar room. Remembering fragments of a dream – a pair of snakes copulating in her lap, a sacrifice she refused to make which led to the spilling of blood and the appearance of enraged female administrators of justice with swollen stomachs and dirty bare feet. On the wall opposite the bed, among the eggshell plaster cracks, the spindrift of dust and whorls of spiderwebs, she sees or fancies she sees the outline of a man's face, a stern, rather pained face with a reproachful look. For a moment she succumbs to the notion that it's Seed's face and that he is stealing his way inside her thoughts and will soon begin speaking inside her mind.

Later she tells Beth about Zivko terrifying the life out of her with his mask.

"That's probably because you tried to cheat," Beth says.

Katie laughs at the absurdity of it all. She vents all her scorn for these games. Then she remembers Seed might be listening to her and stops herself.

"I spent the night on Second Life," Beth says. 'All the girls in the tribe were asking why you haven't been around for a while."

"I logged on earlier but hardly anyone was online."

Katie has studied closely the notecard with all the role playing and conversation with Bysshe Artaud. She's now sure it wasn't her ex-boyfriend Charlie. There was no trace in Bysshe of Charlie's bitterness, of his aggrieved sanctimony. Bysshe was also more playful, more imaginative than Charlie. She has run through a mental list of friends of her mother for possible candidates. She has googled the name Bysshe and discovered it was the middle name of Shelley. Reaffirming her instinct that Bysshe is a man. She was pumping herself high on one of the garden's swings this afternoon, returning her body to a childhood sensation, when the idea rose in her mind that Bysshe might be her father. She read the notecard again with this notion in mind. It was difficult to believe Bysshe's handler was a man in his fifties and he certainly bore no resemblance to any father she had imagined for herself. But, once or twice, Bysshe seemed to display a deferential indulgence towards her, a pressing eagerness to strike up intimacy which might be interpreted as paternal in nature. *Bysshe Artaud takes the hand and caresses it, feeling the heat of the female's blood become part of her own warmth and wellbeing. She finds herself trying to picture the child this girl once was.* It suddenly became plausible in her mind that Bysshe might be her father. She found herself blushing when she reread some of the things she said to what might be her father. And she found she was angry with him for deceiving her. She thought about the resulting impoverishment of never having experienced herself as the daughter of a detailed responsive father. All the memories they had never made together. An entire secret life he hadn't allowed her to live. But then she smiled, a smile that spread warmth throughout her entire being, that he had helped her escape from a cage and that the first thing she said to him was, *Come closer, girl.*

Back out in the garden, sitting cross-legged by her magnolia tree, she dismissed the idea that Bysshe might be her father as ridiculous, just another illustration of her wishful thinking. But while she sat stroking the bark of her tree, thinking aloud, she found the idea would not be so easily discarded.

"Can we unblock that avatar I accused of harassing me? I think I might have made a mistake," she says to Beth.

"I'll do it now," she says.

Katie too logs on. She sends Bysshe Artaud a friend request.

After communal dinner in the refectory Seed forbids all

electric light. Everyone walks around holding a candle. Throwing skittish monstrous shadows on the high walls. Katie, holding a bottle of red wine in one hand, a candle dripping hot wax onto her skin in the other hand, gravitates towards the source of the music. She has just checked her emails. Bysshe Artaud hasn't responded to her friend request. It's a disappointment that has its own complex inner life.

It crosses Katie's mind as she enters the large upstairs room lit by dozens of candles that for the first time since childhood she possesses no house key in her bag. It's a thought that makes the weights in her body dissolve. To shut a front door behind her on an empty home and then realise she might have forgotten her house key is like the definition of panic to her. It has happened to her more than once – she is always misplacing her keys, just as she is always forgetting her passwords. She feels locked out tonight and that it's Bysshe Artaud, maybe her father, who has the key which will enable her to return to her life.

Edgar sits on the floor playing the guitar. Tonight it requires a little effort to convince herself he communicates for her an idea of protection, an embrace of wide understanding. He plays the guitar with an intense self-absorbed air, as if trying to articulate the hidden meaning of his life. She sits down on a sofa between Hunter and Imisa who has wet hair, is barefooted and wrapped only in a green towel.

"You look strangely virginal in the candlelight," says Hunter, his eyes eager and searching. He reaches out and puts his hand on her neck.

"You have no idea how many times I've lost my virginity," she says, tossing back her head in a pantomime pose. "Every time I stand examining myself in a full-length mirror I am the new bride, the virginal spouse, pretending to know less than I'm willing to concede."

"Do you have to be so damn clever all the time?"

"I still haven't forgiven you for abandoning me in the woods."

"You've heard Rodrigo never returned? No one has a clue where he is."

"Zivko probably scared him to death. Or murdered him. No doubt his corpse is now buried in a shallow grave." She no longer cares if Seed is listening. In fact, she rather hopes he is.

"There's some suspicion he might have been an undercover cop."

"Pretty shit at his job then, seeing as he bolted only a week into his assignment."

"I hope you've been keeping your tree entertained," says Hunter. "I saw you earlier talking to it."

"I was telling it it might end up as the paper of a bible or a murder mystery novel. Or else a diary. And then thinking how strange it is that every tree is a potential diary. That's not what I'd call a profitable transaction. Especially when I remember the melodramatic bilge I used to write in my diary. I feel like I ought to beg forgiveness, on my hands and knees, of the tree that was killed to provide the pages of my teenage diary. It's probably one of our most damning conceited delusions that we believe what us humans have to say for ourselves is more important than what trees have to say. Unless, I suppose, you're Leonardo or Virginia Woolf."

Furio now causes a stir by carrying an inflated sex doll into the room. The startled expression on her open mouth makes everyone laugh. After some communal jesting Edgar lays aside his guitar which, Katie knows, once belonged to his best friend who died of a drug overdose. He picks up the garish silicone doll and lays her down on the flagstones of the large room, near the fireplace where a candle illuminates a small pile of feathery ashes. He begins taking off his clothes. First his shoes and socks, then his t-shirt, then his jeans. He has everyone's heightened attention. He strips down to his shorts. He has dirty feet, Katie notices, baffled like everyone else what he's up to. He kneels over the spread-eagled doll and begins caressing her small breasts. "The female nipple," he says, in a loud television documentary voice, "is an electric blue nerve that connects to the deepest part of the womb. To be touched, caressed, kissed here lights up this nerve to its brightest intensity and generates a humming shiver throughout the body. Small sparks travel up and down inside the woman's body, awakening deep slumbering sensations within. Waves begin to swirl inside her most secret places. Let's move down," he says. "Now, as I touch her, I feel her pleasure spread like sunlight over the surface of her skin. The clitoris is like a clematis in essence. Or a rose with lots of petals protecting the heart of the flower. The clitoris is pink and shines and if you allow your fingers to run up and down and around it will respond by swelling and getting harder and bigger. These inner lips or folds I'm running my mouth over now are called the labia and each woman is unique and different in colour, texture and size. Observe now," he says, turning to face his audience, "the mist of surrender in her blue eyes. A little further down is the urethra which is tiny and difficult to see and that's where urine is passed. Then there's the vaginal opening which is surrounded by bits of pink tissue that are the vestiges of the hymen. When I curl my fingers inside her they encounter the spongy texture of the tissue which when touched always make her gasp. I lick at her clitoris, enjoying the taste of her secretions on my tongue. I am reminded of the privacy and intimacy of rain. I feel myself sink down further into a dark resourceful embrace, a sticky coalescence."

He turns to face his audience, catching Imisa's eye, gets to his feet and takes a bow.

When the applause dies down there's an atmosphere in the room, unless she's imagining it, that an orgy is only one whisper distant. It's on the tip of her tongue to suggest it herself. She has had a threesome, but never an orgy. She doubts if she would enjoy it except as an anecdote, but anecdotes are important to her. They are missives of identity, prestige, celebration. Seed himself has already become for her an accumulation of riveting anecdotes which she imagines delivering up at some dinner party in the future. She likes to think of herself as the teller of entertaining stories. It's one of her ways of claiming limelight.

Thus her tendency is often to exaggerate the gifts and uniqueness of the people she knows, in order to make them more compelling as characters in her stories. For this reason she has a talent for making people feel good about themselves. Never letting on that they are the background of a bigger story, her story.

She is trying to bring under control her jealousy that Edgar has sat down next to Imisa when she is called to the confessional. She walks through the echoing maze of interconnected rooms with her candle. Her shadow on the walls is misshapen, volatile and dwarfing. In a corridor she meets Zivko, also carrying a candle. She shrinks from him. He greets her with the faintest of nods. She supposes he has just been in the confessional, though she never hears his name summoned over the speakers. As if he and Seed share some secret means of communication.

This time there is no image of her father amongst the film projected on the wall of the small vaulted room. Tonight every splice of footage in the montage runs backwards at breakneck speed. It makes her feel disorientated, dizzy. Then Seed begins to speak.

"Much of what we think of as sanity is merely impersonation. Mother sets an example. Father lays down the law. Every moment of every day. The formation of a surface. And when composition begins inspiration is already on the decline. There are victories and defeats. We are the brave. We are the frightened. We bow. We clap. We apologise. We read what's written on the page. We repeat after them. I will do the same for you. To your faults be true."

Seed, she realises, has put a lot of work into making his voice hypnotic. It also strikes her how polite his voice is, almost ingratiating. Once again she tries to imagine what he looks like. She prides herself in being skilled at reading the history of a face. Denying everyone his face, she suspects, is how he acquires power.

"Why is everyone here, Katie? You're all here because you've refused every future on offer to you. You want something more, something better. You believe you're worthy of something better, something more."

"You've already said this to me."

He doesn't reply.

"I guess it must be difficult remembering what you've already said to each individual," she says, emboldened by the angry fallout of the two disappointments she has suffered from men tonight. "Do you tailor your words to the person you're talking to or just say the same stuff to everyone?"

"Most of our life consists of elapsed time, Katie. If we could watch it back we'd be bored out of our minds. The minutes seem like hours. The hours seem like days. The days seem like years. Even sex, sometimes a glowing milestone, can be mundane. Just another function of the body. Even sex can lose its power to create secrets. Except, now and again, we are part of a moment that has exalting regenerative power."

She wonders if he's reading from a pre-prepared script.

"I have decided to trust you, Katie. It's a step into the dark to trust someone. It's 1997. I am living in Eugene, Oregon. There are forty beautiful heritage trees due to be cut down to make way for a parking lot outside the offices of a large corporation. Lots of residents aren't happy. Including me. A public hearing is called where citizens will be able to raise their objections to the city council. Except the city announces they are going to cut down the trees the day before the meeting. Eleven people climb up into the trees to prevent the murder. To stave off the killing of these beautiful living repositories of our heritage and our health for twenty-four hours, until the public hearing. The police arrive wearing riot gear and gas masks. Law enforcement officers are lifted up in fire truck buckets and begin pepper spraying the protestors in the trees. They cut the trouser-legs of the protestors up to the groin so they can spray pepper on their private parts. The protestors in the trees scream out in agonies of discomfort. They are hanging precariously from the branches. I am in the crowd. I am tear gassed in the face. I have never before felt hate like I do now for the officer behind his visor who sprays my face with scalding pepper. There's nothing I want more than to do him grievous bodily harm. But I have to silence my voice. I have to embrace my impotence. I have no more autonomy than a child. The protestors brave it out for six hours. Then all the beautiful living trees are murdered. They are brought crashing to the ground. This is the day I am radicalised.

"It isn't long before I participate in my first protest action. There is a company that rounds up wild horses from government land. The horses are sent to a slaughterhouse, to make dog food. This company is processing so many horses that blood often overwhelms the town's water treatment facility and shuts it down. Local residents have been protesting for years. We creep into the facility at night and burn it to the ground. The company never recovers and has to shut down. In one night we have achieved what the local residents had failed to do in ten years. We then firebomb a plant that is dumping toxic waste into a local water supply. Then comes Seattle. Protesting the WTO. It is mostly non-violent civil disobedience. But we have other ideas. We vandalise every corporation building we can find. It feels good to take out my rage on corporation windows. But by now the FBI is channelling a lot of its resources into a manhunt for us and more than once I suspect an individual on the fringe of things of being an FBI infiltrator. We are branded as terrorists. Like the Black Panthers before us. Even though not one single individual is ever harmed in any of our actions. So I come to France.

"It seems to me, Katie, that you're able to believe whatever is necessary to extract the most sensation from the moment. I like this in you. You have the ability to channel all of yourself into the present moment. The moment of now. Reality has to be invented. I think you know this. All artists know this. We have to create it ourselves. Otherwise it's only what happens to us, what we're constrained to endure.

"Which brings us to the moment of now. There's a Lakota

reservation in North and South Dakota where my wife grew up. An oil pipeline is presently being constructed under sacred burial land and underneath the Mississippi river. There's a high risk of the region's drinking water becoming polluted. This is land given to the Lakota in a government treaty. Protestors there who have chained themselves to the rape and pillage machinery are pepper sprayed in the eyes, including old men and women."

Passing before her eyes now is jittery footage of an old Lakota woman whose face is crosshatched with deep grooves. She has chained herself to a piece of machinery. A law enforcement officer with bulging thighs is holding back her head while trying to prise open her screwed shut eyes with his fat fingers. A sense of his character is conveyed to Katie from his posture, from his rough insensitive hands, from the stiff truculent way his head sits on his neck. She catches a glimpse of the kind of life he might lead. The kind of life that would mean death to her. The kind of life that ought to mean death to any woman. And yet any daughter he might have would no doubt love him. It is too easy, she thinks, for a father to inspire love in a daughter. Another of biology's crude commands.

A second officer, down on his knees, seen from behind, swabs the woman's left eye with some kind of chemical solution. There is a grotesque look of terror on the old woman's face. She tries to shake her head back and forth but the first officer's grip is tight. The second officer applies the swab to her other eye. The woman's cheeks are damp with the stuff. An asthmatic series of sobs rack her old body. Katie is shocked into horrified silence by what she's watching. As much as anything by the unfeeling manner in which the two men perform this act of torture.

"Don't you want to kill those two police officers, Katie? What you're watching is Nazi policy in action. Remember that image tomorrow night. One of the men responsible is holidaying not far from here. Tomorrow night you're going to his house. You will wear dark clothes. Zivko will tell you what to do when you get inside. And take a knife."

10

For three hours Katie sits in the back of the van with Hunter, Dodo and Imisa. Zivko is driving. She sits wrapped up in her own arms, as if miming loneliness. Bysshe Artaud has still not accepted her friendship request. She now feels aggrieved to be forced offline for the entire day and night. There is sometimes too much privacy inside the van and she is made to feel how little hoarded intimacy she has to draw on with her companions. When she expresses her misgivings about what they are doing, Hunter tells her to chill out. "We're just going to create some mischief."

"The guy we're paying a visit to is responsible for more pollution to the planet than entire countries," says Dodo. She seems to be flaunting more piercings today and has dyed her hair green. "Entire civilisations, come to that."

"What are we going to do, exactly?"

"Don't worry. Probably you'll just be on look-out duty."

"And what the fuck are the knives for?"

"Did you bring a knife?"

"No."

Hunter begins tickling her. She cavorts about under his prying hands, her body twisting into wild ungainly shapes, her protests acquiring a note of hysteria.

It's night when the van pulls to a halt and Zivko lets them out. Katie's hair is stirred faintly by a breath of salted sea air. The smell of the sea is always to her a summons to adventure. They are standing on a high coastal road with hanging arabesques of flowering vines which sweetly perfume the air. Stored heat comes up through the soles of her feet from the tarmac. Down below the black sweep of the Mediterranean is broken here and there by braids of phosphorescent silver. Katie's eye goes to the yellow lights of a silhouetted tanker at anchor on the horizon and then to the half-moon up in the darkening firmament.

Led by Zivko, they descend single file down a narrow alley-way of steep uneven steps. Sand crunches beneath her canvas shoes. The darkness deepens into billowing black smoke. The night air is thick with hoarded scent. She turns a corner and beneath a host of stars is once more face to face with the sweep of the open sea. The waves uncoil with a serpent hiss over the fossilised rocks. She watches the golden moon shiver on the black water. Then, following Zivko and Hunter, she jumps from rock to rock, and feels her body consent to the virginal poise of the world around her.

They sit down on an outcrop of tiered rocks flanking a small secluded bay. Behind them is the high wall of a large sequestered villa. Zivko tells them they have to wait another hour. No one says much. As if they are all on their own now. Katie feels the markings of the sharp fossil-encrusted rocks against which her hands are pressed imprint themselves on her palms. Waves can be heard plunging in and out of hidden crevices below. Fugitive grains of light carried in on the tide are dragged back by the undertow into the hypnotic heave of the sea.

Zivko tells everyone to put on their gloves and balaclavas and to make sure there are no prints on their knives. What little he says is delivered in a surly and automated tone. He never emerges from behind his disgruntled, embittered air. He puts on his own gloves and then takes from his rucksack a knife and the horned animal mask. He puts on the mask. He lights his face from beneath with the torch and looks at her just as he did out on the country road when he had frightened her half to death. A fume of madness enters the atmosphere. She feels it snake into her bloodstream. There is a nervous flutter in the pit of her stomach, a change in her glandular secretions, like the beginning in the blood of an amphetamine drug. A black void swirls and sucks at the back of her thoughts which have become louder, as if she is standing in a stark place of origin. She watches everyone put on black gloves and a black balaclava. She does the same.

In the torchlight gossamer reflections from the sea ripple over the villa's wall like spirit maps. She notices an overhead security camera attached to a post. Hunter helps her hoist her weight up onto the rugged narrow ledge of the wall. She perches there for a moment, remaining stock still, her eye drawn to the progress of the thin jumpy beam of Zivko's torch. She jumps down into the garden with a dull thud which goes on reverberating up through the soles of her feet. There is a rustling in the undergrowth beneath a pair of sharp-needled evergreen trees. She hears the thud behind her of Hunter landing on the lawn. She walks towards the villa with a sensation of being blindfolded. Holding out her arms to help with her balance, as if she is walking the plank of a pirate ship. She is struck by how much effort simplicity can sometimes demand. Her heart is pounding in her ears. She chronicles the world entirely with her senses. There is a rectangular glow of lighter darkness which she identifies as a covered swimming pool. She feels like she is leaving indelible marks on the earth behind her, as if this entire area will become a crime scene. And that this moment has already become a kind of dream she will be unable to leave in the future.

Her face is hot under the balaclava. Her skin mottled and irritated. Her body prickling with heightened awareness, as if possessed by some nocturnal feral creature. In the darkness every tremor of movement creates a stutter of suspense in which she feels both exposed and causal.

She sees an apparition of herself, wearing the balaclava, on dark glass. Her ghost sends a searing bolt of unreality through her. Never before has she been so unrecognisable to herself. She watches Zivko ease an outer door open. The click of the yielding latch detonates in some chamber of her mind like the retort of a gun. She follows Imisa, stepping lightly into a high spacious sitting room where the smell of dying lilies is overwhelming. The knife Imisa holds intermittently glints in the thin torchlight. The sense of people sleeping on the floor above is a palpable part of the moment. Their innocence at this moment. Their blissful ignorance of the fact there are crazy people with knives in their house. Katie now knows she has become a crazy person. She has the sensation the world inside her mind is breaking asunder from the world outside her mind and she is unable to locate herself in either.

She recalls the seasoned face, like brown parchment, of the old Lakota woman in the film. She needs to feel some hate for the people in this house. Needs to believe they deserve this nightmare intrusion into the ease and entitlement of their life. She recalls the law enforcement officer on his knees, smearing chemicals on the old woman's eyes. His conscientious unfeeling concentration, as if he was administering not pain but first aid.

Zivko and Dodo reappear with handfuls of bottles and food packages from the kitchen. Zivko puts the torch down on a low table and its beam slices a furrow of watery light through the darkness. Katie watches them begin emptying the bottles of sauce and bleach on the furniture and rugs. Dodo squirts tomato ketchup over the white wall by the fireplace. The squelching hiss the squeezed plastic bottle makes is as loud as a thunderclap to Katie's ears. She is poised to bolt. But she stares dumbfounded at Dodo who is forming letters of the red sauce with her gloved hands. She makes a P, an I, a G, another G, an I, an E and finally a S.

Hunter is disembowelling the cushions on the sofa with his knife. Imisa is cutting to shreds a lilac shawl with her knife. Zivko, in his mask, is now empting bottles of oil and vinegar on the sofa. The sharp tang of the vinegar makes Katie feel like she might sneeze. Dodo is chucking flour everywhere. She empties some of it over her head so her balaclava glows with a kind of snow sheen. Then Zivko motions to Dodo and, following the beam of his torch, they begin creeping up the stairs. They both grip their knives with what Katie reads as laundered intent. She looks to Hunter for reassurance but his eyes inside his mask are riveted to the two figures climbing the stairs. She senses he is no less in the prey of shocked horror than she is. She realises she is grinding her teeth. Imisa says in a hissing whisper that it's time for them to leave.

Katie is skirting the swimming pool when the light appears in an upstairs window. She is suddenly able to see her gloved hands. A piercing female scream leaves a broadening fraught silence in its wake. Katie feels this is a moment that is already acquiring history. Then the scream arrives again, more shrill, more outraged with terror. She thinks she hears a pleading male voice in the spaces between the screams. But perhaps it's something she only imagines.

Nick and Katie

1

"To be honest, I didn't know Nick had a daughter."

"Neither did he until six months ago."

"He would have been a wonderful father, especially to a daughter."

"You're David, aren't you?"

"Your father was the first friend I ever had. He was also the best friend I ever had."

"I wish I had known him."

Katie begins to cry. She allows herself to be held by this man with the long grey hair, beautiful hands and impish eyebrows. What she wants is not comfort though. What she feels she wants is to stand out in gusting rain with an upturned face bleeding mascara and refuse all shelter.

"Did you know there's not one photo of him on the internet in which he's older than about twenty-six and not wearing makeup? It's impossible for me to picture him as a father. Tell me something about him," she says, wiping her streaming nose on the back of her hand.

He looks uncomfortable for a moment, exposed and pitifully vulnerable. Then he composes himself, assumes a kind of professional air. "For me, he was like a favourite song. The kind you already want to hear again before it's ended. He gave me the feeling of protection and belonging and uplift a favourite song gives you. He could foretell me to myself. Very few people have that gift."

"Tell me more," she says. *But not as if you're being interviewed for a magazine article*, she thinks.

"Well, I suppose he always had a cleansing effect on me. Like summer rain. I was never ever bored in his company. You can't say that about many people. And he helped me believe in myself. He extended my horizons. His fingerprints are all over so many of the most cherished moments of my life. He loved to talk. But intimately, in a secluded corner. He hated small talk. And he always made you feel seen when he talked. He brought you to life to yourself. The past can be such a hauntingly beautiful place. It's a wonder sometimes the heart doesn't break into small pieces. I remember one of the first times we tried applying makeup to our faces. It was both a solemn ritual and an occasion of riotous laughter. He always took himself a little less seriously than I did. We fell out, you know. I hadn't seen him since the nineties. I realised when I heard he'd died that I had always expected us to rekindle our bond at some point. That we didn't will probably be the thing I most regret in my life. He's taught me the mind is often divisive, but the heart always knows better. I should have followed my heart more. I think he always did. That's why he would have been an inspiring father."

"It's sad he can't hear you," she says. She catches the eye of her mother who is standing with the priest and Hunter in the churchyard. The empathy and love her mother conveys make her eyes well up again. She fixes her attention back on David. "Why *did* you two fall out?"

"I loathed being a pop star. Being constantly in the public eye. The false perception created of me. My life no longer felt like it was my own. My son suffers from claustrophobia. In his teens he would be on a Tube train with friends and his whole being would be screaming out with the plea to return to the open air. He had no choice but to get off as soon as the doors opened again, in no state to explain to his friends why he was prematurely abandoning them. He was too ashamed of what he thought of as weakness to tell them the truth. He got the reputation of being distant and arrogant. That's how fame affected me. I just couldn't handle it anymore. I had to get out. I had to abandon my friends. I've not once appeared on TV since Orfée broke up. I've barely given any interviews. I've been able to live a quiet life while still making music."

"That doesn't explain why you fell out."

"I need a cigarette. Do you want one?"

Katie accepts the cigarette from the crumpled French soft pack. He lights it for her.

"There's no simple answer to that question. Nick enjoyed being a pop star much more than I did. I knew that. And it was what we had dreamed of as kids so he was right to enjoy it. Once I knew I had to get off that train I suppose I began feeling guilty towards him. As if I was letting him down. As soon as someone begins making you feel guilty or is responsible for any feelings you don't like you begin to turn on them, you begin to distance yourself from them. You have to, to defend yourself. To be honest, I always believed Nick would become successful in his own right after we broke up. It was necessary for my own peace of mind to believe that. Every single bass player I've worked with has expressed his or her admiration for Nick. Everyone always smiles with a glow of affection when they talk about Nick. Then, when ten years had passed and he had vanished from the music scene, I thought about inviting him to play on my next album. But we had always been equals and I found I couldn't comfortably step into the shoes of his employer. It somehow demeaned everything that was true about us. I know I should have been more honest with him. The public story is that I stole his girlfriend. But that isn't true. Him and Giuliana were never more than just friends. That said, I didn't behave well towards him. I know that. But if I could choose three people I'd like to journey with in a next life Nick would be one of them. And I'm pretty sure that if I was in that coffin and he was standing here he'd say the same about me. There's no law that says you have to live forever in the same house with the people you love. In fact, in my experience, it's more of a rarity than a commonplace, that love physically binds people together. In the physical world, love separates more often than it binds. Love is what you carry in your heart, not what you hold in your hands. Strange fateful forces were at work during that period. It never felt like we were in control of what was happening. And if you think about it, two human beings were born as a direct result of decisions made then. You and my son. I wouldn't want to change that."

The woman who sat beside David in the church now walks over.

"This is my ex-wife Giuliana."

"Your speech in there was beautiful. It moved us both to tears. Your father was a beautiful and very special man."

"Thank you." These are the first two famous people Katie has ever met. (She watches a YouTube video of a Pina Bausch choreography when she gets home. There is Giuliana, at the height of her beauty, not the wizened tired woman with the sagging face and dull hair Katie meets, one of several dancers in pastel coloured dresses, throwing buckets of water over each other on a beautifully lit stage and making impossibly bewitching shapes of her body.) She likes to think it's a signal of some depth change in her that she feels no desire to be photographed with them.

When she rejoins her mother she experiences a sense of solidarity and shared warmth that is also new.

"The priest told me he remembers seeing your father on *Top of the Pops*. Who would have thought priests watched *Top of the Pops*? We have no idea what goes on in people's lives, do we? So you met David?"

"He was nice."

"He looks so old. It's sad. It doesn't suit him, being old. But then I don't feel it suits me either."

"He talked more about himself than about my dad."

"It's good you call him your dad."

"I call him that so I might one day be able to feel it."

"And you met the femme fatale. She's the dancer your father was in love with. She caused all the bitterness when she betrayed him for David. He told me he once paid her a surprise visit at her parents' home up in the mountains of the Molise. It took him thirty-six hours to get there. Are they coming for a drink?"

"I don't know. I didn't ask." Katie takes her phone from her bag and turns it back on. "He took all the credit for me getting born."

"What do you mean?"

"He said had he not made the decision to break up the band you and Dad would never have met."

"That's probably true."

"How did you meet? I've never asked."

"He stopped me on the street and asked for directions. I pretended not to recognise him even though I had all his records. But I was in love with David. In a silly girlish way I mean. He was looking for an art supplies shop. He wanted clay. Luckily I knew where it was because I liked to paint in those days."

"I didn't know you ever painted."

"Watercolours. I wasn't very good but I enjoyed it. And that's what we talked about. Art. I couldn't believe it when he asked for my phone number. So David's right. It's almost certainly true that your father wouldn't have been on that street looking for clay and you wouldn't have got born had he and David not fallen out. He'd probably have been touring Japan or appearing on TV in Australia."

A foothold above all the waste and heartbreak is that her father tried to contact her the moment he found out about her. Her mother told her about his quest to track her down in the virtual world of Second Life. "He hired a private investigator in there to find you!" She has read through the transcript of their interactions countless times. The only conversation she ever had with her father, the only adventure they shared. Her attention always so heightened, so charged with wonder, it's as if she is puzzling out coded script on ancient parchment. Why, she has wondered countless times, didn't you just tell me who you were? She's impressed though at the mischievous lengths he went to in his roleplaying to engage her. It suggests he would have been able to fully enter the spirit of any game. That aspect of fatherhood, at least, he would have excelled at. She knows it will always be a wasteland in her life that he never allowed her to see herself through his eyes, that he gave her no opportunity to learn the things he knew. But at least he has exonerated himself of some of the blame. After she fled from Seed's community with Hunter, following the insane night at the villa, she continued to hope Bysshe would accept her friend request. She understands now he was by then riddled with the cancer that killed him in only three months.

A month ago she learned Seed was arrested. Accused of firebombing a meat packing plant and a timber company. There was a photo of him online in handcuffs between two towering law enforcement agents with wires in their ears. He is a small rumpled man with little obvious charisma. Along with him thirteen other members of the family were arrested, including Dodo, Beth, Raine, Furio, Edgar, Imisa and Zivko. All except Zivko have agreed to become cooperating witnesses in exchange for a reduced sentence. There was no mention of Sadie. She also learned the man whose villa they vandalised suffered a heart attack that night brought on by the sight of Zivko standing in his bedroom wearing the horned animal mask and wielding a knife. It wasn't though a fatal heart attack. And she feels no sympathy for him after reading what his oil corporation is doing to the planet.

"Those two women talking to David were fans of the band," says her mother now. "They've come all the way from Durham."

Hunter is holding Katie's hand. She though is thinking of the magnolia sapling. The most beautiful legacy of her time with Seed. She articulated hopes before her tree, worked on doubts and often found herself thinking of her father while touching its trunk under the stars. She can feel its grainy texture on her fingertips now. It both gladdens and saddens her that it will carry on growing without her. She will never tell anyone the location of her tree. She wants to think of it as the secret she shares with her father.

Sam

2

The aim of the annual school concert is to raise awareness of the catastrophic perils caused by global warming. Students have painted posters which hang all around the assembly hall. They have drawn diagrams and statistical charts. They have compiled montages of photographs.

Sam is now on the stage under the lights. His recently formed band are playing three songs, the last of which is Orfée's 'Scorched Earth'. Finally he has mastered the bass part and all its difficult phrasing. The news of Nick Swallow's death he experienced as a personal loss. He discovered there existed in him a hope they would one day become friends. He would like to dedicate this concert to Nick Swallow, except when he imagines announcing this into the microphone it seems absurdly presumptuous of him to dedicate something so amateurish and insignificant to the memory of someone so gifted and inspirational.

The sick churning feeling in his stomach when he walked out on stage is replaced by a quiet sweeping sense of elation half way through the first song. He now never wants this moment to end. His one regret is that his grandmother is not here to see him.

She has been put in a care home. He protested the decision. And was made to feel a child with no knowledge of the decrees and priorities of the adult world. He went to see her yesterday after school. She was sitting in an armchair in a large lounge of childish colours with all the other broken old people, mostly women. Her hair had been tied back into a ponytail, which struck him as the kind of humiliation she would never have allowed in better times. He also noticed she wasn't wearing her favourite ring which she always turned around and around on her finger as if it gave her comfort. There was nowhere for him to sit so he had to crouch down in front of her. He spoke to her of her achievements as a ballerina. He reminded her of Sadler Wells and Margot Fontaine and Swan Lake. He hummed the opening bars of the dance of the swans. He wanted to take her back to her native ground. He wanted to reanimate a memory of all the beauty she created in the past. And he wanted everyone in the room to know about the gifts she had once possessed. (It pains him that there doesn't exist a single piece of film of her dancing.) She looked at him with a blank stare and a polite smile, as if he was trying to sell her something she didn't have any need of. There was no light of recognition in her eyes. His presence began to agitate the old man sitting in the adjacent armchair. Sam didn't therefore stay long. As he was leaving he turned around and took a last look at her sitting in her armchair. He has never seen anyone look so alone and unreachable. Tears welled up behind his eyes and he was embarrassed and quickly left the care home. He thinks of that moment now as when he received the touch of a ghost.

When they finish 'Scorched Earth' the hall erupts in a crescendo of noise. Sam turns to Jon, sitting behind his drum kit. They exchange a smile. Jones has now become Jon. Sam still marvels at the moment, in music class, he discovered his old nemesis harbours the ambition to be a drummer. He now often goes to Jon's house with his bass guitar and they practise together. He has even got Jon to share his love of Orfée. Five Nancy boys who wore makeup and coloured their hair. One time they laughed about the names Jon used to call Sam and the day he stole Sam's shoe. And Sam afterwards came to appreciate how powerful are the healing and uniting properties of music and why music is considered the universal language. While feeding his fox he understands the natural world too is held together by its music. Even if at times you can't hear it, you can feel it in the pulse of your blood if you listen closely.

It was Jon who suggested they finish the set with 'Scorched Earth'. They both struggled to master their parts. But because the song's title was so appropriate for the concert's theme they knew they had to give it their best shot.

Out in the crowd Sam sees Jamil, his other best friend. He is on his feet, clapping and hollering. No one anymore refers to him as a terrorist. And he sees Waseem too. Even Warlow and Dixon, marginalised figures without the patronage of Jon Jones, are applauding.

Acknowledgements

For inspiration, sustenance and feedback, thanks to: Charles Cecil, Freddie de Rougemont, Georgiana Calthorpe, Mick Karn, David Sylvian, Emily Pennock, VJ Keegan, Steve Jansen, Richard Barbieri, Rob Dean, Rupert Alexander, Justin Sparrow, Anna von Kanitz, Pina Bausch, Jessica St. James, Talitha Stevenson, Paola Rosà, Gina Monaco, Tim Binding, Alex Preston, Judith Kinghorn, Annabel Merullo, Charlie Campbell, Hamid Khanbhai, Christabel Brudnell-Bruce, Charlotte Raymond, David Flusfeder, Tim Atkins, Eloise Anson, Vanessa Garwood, Hugo Wilson, Antonia Barclay, Lucy Corbett, Tom Lumley, Tiarnan McCarthy, Sarah Haybittle, Chiara De Cabarrus, Kim Macconnell, Rachel Webster, Stuart Bridgeman, Linda Fleischman, Linda Thomas, Kerrie Ashworth, Paolo Cristellotti, Katie St. George, Ebba Heuman, Cristina Zamagni.

CPSIA information can be obtained
at www.ICGtesting.com
Printed in the USA
BVHW08025251021
619820BV00010B/363

9 781999 968267